C000256520

DARK EDGE PRESS

ISBN: 9798684847165

Printed and bound by Usk River Publishing
Newport,
Wales.

# BURIED SINS

## LOUISE MULLINS

# FULL DESCRIPTION

When Carys returns to her childhood home, inherited after the death of her father, she is shocked to discover the bones of an infant buried in the paddock. Days later, DI Locke's team uncover the remains of a missing girl, sparking vivid memories of the day Carys was abducted by The Shadow Man.

While the evidence against her father mounts, Carys recalls more of her past. And each new revelation provides DI Locke with the proof she needs to close the cases of several girls' disappearances.

Sometimes the past refuses to stay buried.

# ADVANCED READER REVIEWS

'Ambiguous characters, a creepily plausible plot, and a bone chilling story set in the welsh valleys. Leaves the reader with a constant sense of doom as they turn the pages to reach the most dramatic and dark of conclusions'

# Ty Mynydd, Llangynidr Road, Brynmawr, Ebbw Vale, Wales

*Thursday 9th February 1994*

There was no way anyone could know the soil and wet leaves of the freshly dug earth covered a body, but Bryn knew because he'd buried it.

He turned away from the window when he heard a key in the lock and moved from the sink toward the door, plastering a neutral expression on his face, acting as if everything was fine. He even managed to boil the kettle, pour two cups of tea, and join in with conversation. But while he sat at the dining table facing his spouse his sight was constantly drawn toward the window to the garden wall, where beyond it, in the paddock, lay a corpse buried four feet below ground surrounded by rubble and fallen branches. The mound visible only if you stood at the right angle

1

or knew what the earth contained.

Pain jolted him from his thoughts. There were teeth marks indented on the skin around his finger, the nail bitten too close to the flesh. He moved his hand from his mouth and prayed Carys couldn't see beneath his nerves and into his demonic soul.

Bryn's daughter didn't question why he wasn't there to collect her from school. And so, he thought he'd got away with it.

# PART ONE

# CARYS

*Brynmawr, Ebbw Vale, Wales, 2018*

I found the bones as I was clearing out the garden. The ground was waterlogged from a burst sewerage pipe, the paddock flooded. I stood with my Wellingtons slouched in inches of mud that had turned into an oily sludge as it passed through the irrigation system before spurting from the weed-riddled, overgrown grass.

The house was cluttered. Thick mould lined the walls of the attic where my father kept the memorabilia of my youth. Photograph albums were scattered around, boxes were stacked up covering the length and breadth of the wooden slatted floor. The low beams and lack of sunlight or air – my father having never fitted a Velux window into the attic – gave the large spacious room a cramped, dingy look.

The place had a musty smell and left a dark cloak of foreboding to fall over me as I entered.

'You weren't joking when you said he liked to hoard stuff,' said Lewis, my husband of eighteen years.

I glanced around the place and felt the hairs on my arms rise along with the swathes of discomfort I felt at being inside my childhood home for the first time in twenty years, surrounded by sharp awful memories and an unsettling feeling in my stomach as I treaded over piles of rubbish.

I took one last glance around the room then moved toward the hatch. 'I'm going back downstairs, are you coming?'

Lewis followed me down, but Rhys stayed, finding interest in an old fax machine my father used to send invoices to his clients with, after he brought the accountancy firms office home with him.

I heard his voice in the back of my head, 'home-based business is where it's at now, Rhiannon.' My mother looked at him and smiled warmly, shaking her head at his latest idea to make 'big money' without having to leave the farm. But it worked, much to her surprise. Hence that was probably how he came to afford all the stuff he'd filled the house with over the years preceding her death.

The stairs were cluttered too with piles of washing ready to be taken into the laundry room that had never made it there before he'd keeled over. The washing machine was housed in the small square space I passed as I ambled around downstairs looking for something to do before feeling my feet grow heavy and my head spin as I passed the downstairs broom cupboard.

As I was about to dip into the kitchen in search of something to clean the kettle with, so we could have a cuppa there was a loud knock on the thick wooden front door. I crossed the hall and opened it to a red-haired woman in her sixties wearing a deep vermillion coloured summer coat over a tight fitted floral dress that looked far too expensive to be seen out wearing in the country. She looked out of place. I stifled a laugh.

'Gwenda,' she said, holding out a bunch of keys. She fingered them and named each individually as Lewis appeared in the doorway behind me. 'Shed, barn, garage, stables, basement.'

'Basement?'

She went stiff but didn't reply.

I couldn't remember there being a basement in the property.

'You must be my father's neighbour,' I said.

She nodded.

I gathered she was more than that when she'd called to inform me of his passing. I wasn't surprised when she told me he hired her as his home-help. Unless paid, no one would want to be in my father's company. Though looking at her I had a hard job seeing past her stony demeanour wondering what possessed my father to employ her.

*Maybe she's not the neighbour*, said a voice in the back of my head. *How do you even know she's Gwenda? You've never even met the woman.*

'I kept an eye on Bryn, and the house after he . . .'

She was the one who found him. Dead in his armchair in front of the television, a plate of dried uneaten food in front of him, a three-day-old newspaper opened on the sports page lying across the armrest. A heart attack, the coroner said.

'Thank you, for . . .' *Finding him? Informing me of his death? Dealing with the funeral when I told you I couldn't make it? Not questioning why his only*

7

*daughter wanted nothing to do with him for two decades? Attending the will reading? Although you were left a substantial amount of money, I didn't want a penny of it, not even for compensatory purposes. For the keys?* '. . . everything.'

'Yes, well, I did what I had to.'

Lewis smiled at her, but she didn't reciprocate.

Bryn kept himself to himself. His house was his kingdom. He would have hated his estranged daughter charging into his home, manhandling his prized possessions, and throwing stuff out. So why had he allowed Gwenda into his private sanctuary?

I smiled, pleased with myself for disturbing the place my father, Bryn Howell, kept so untidy it was difficult to see anything of worth amongst the mountains of crap he'd accumulated in the years since I left.

'It was my job.'

'Yes.' I couldn't think of anything else to say to the stranger stood in front of me who seemed to know the layout of the farm better than I could remember.

After an awkward pause, she said, 'we should talk sometime. I'm a quarter of a mile down the lane.' Then she turned sharply and left.

I closed the door, brushed the ripped, blackened net curtain aside and peered through the murky glass to see her wander down the path while looking up at the roof, missing a few tiles. I followed her eyes down to the kitchen window nestled above the basement. An area of the house I didn't know existed until that day. My eyes fell to the key in my hand.

'Let's go and have a look,' said Lewis.

I reluctantly followed Lewis back through the house to what I'd always believed was the broom cupboard, wondering why my father felt compelled to lie to me, and to lock it.

Lewis forced the key into the hole, it jammed tight. He wiggled it a bit then it *clunked*. The door swung wide and slammed against the wall, forcing out a blast of cold dusty air onto my face.

Lewis switched on the light. It flickered into life, dimmed to an orange glow, then died.

'We'll have to get some energy saving bulbs in here or this place is going to cost a fortune in electricity while we're doing it up,' said Lewis, holding out his phone to the pitch-dark basement, the torch function casting a bright white beacon of light across the concrete floor.

I noted the wires fed up through the bare floorboards and plugged into sockets for appliances we hadn't yet figured out the locations of. 'We should probably get the electrics PAT-tested too. I doubt this place has been rewired since my grandfather lived here.'

Lewis ran his hand down the wall and damp paper came away at his fingertips. 'It needs a lot of work.'

The decorating wouldn't start until we'd renovated the place, and we couldn't even begin that until we'd thrown out or burnt the shit my father had collected over the years.

The farm was dismal and depressing no matter how much paint you slapped against the walls, but there were also structural issues that demanded immediate attention. Just thinking about it made my head swirl. There were at least two bedrooms I knew needed re-plastering, and thick chunks of it had come away from the walls of the passageway downstairs, leaving a crumbling mess to line the floor.

I did a three-sixty, something beckoning me to circle the basement I couldn't remember living above. Surely, those were the things children never forgot: spooky doorways that led down to frighteningly dark cellars?

My father was the kind of man who would have tortured me with tales of goblins and bogeymen waiting in the dark to jump out and frighten me to death. If the basement had been in use when I was a little girl, I had no doubt he would have threatened to lock me in there at some point. Or perhaps he had, and that was why I was selectively seeking no memory of it.

I walked carefully down the stone-cold steps and into the thirty-six by twenty-eight square foot concrete basement. There were sheets covering everything from broken ornaments and rusty tools to smashed crockery and old kitchen utensils.

A knot of anxiety wove itself around my stomach at the sight of a mattress leaning against the wall for some peculiar reason, though I couldn't understand why.

I sifted through piles of Awake! magazines lining the walls, compelled to investigate the contents of some plastic containers my mother once used to sell at Tupperware parties before her friends stopped speaking to her.

A fleeting shadow descended on me and I looked

up to find Lewis stood over my shoulder watching as I opened the lid of one to reveal a dead spider. 'How did it get in there?' he said.

'Maybe grandpa collected insects,' said Rhys from the doorway, a mischievous grin on his face. Always the one to invoke discussion on the macabre.

Did he? No, I didn't think so. But then I couldn't trust my own memory, could I? Not if I didn't have any before the age of twelve.

For the next five minutes I moved lazily around the room while Lewis, at my instruction, picked up the boxes without looking at what was inside, carried them out of the basement, down the passageway, and through the front door. Dumping them on the ground outside ready for the first of what I understood would be dozens of trips to the rubbish tip.

'We're going to need a skip.'

I gave Lewis a look that said, 'I told you so,' and he reached out and pulled me close. I sunk my face into his chest, breathed in his familiar masculine scent and steadied myself, preparing for another bout of tears. I'd cried many since receiving the phone call from Gwenda, informing me of my father's death, releasing all the pent-up anger and resentment I'd contained for years.

'I found your number on the website,' she said. 'You're still doing it then?'

She meant photography. I guessed my father had spoken about me to *some* people over the years. Gwenda it appeared was one of them.

'Talked about you a lot, he did,' she said, accusingly, as though it was my fault my mother had got sick and died, and my father was left to live on his own once I had the courage to leave home.

'I bet he never told you why I left?' I wanted to say. Instead I held my tongue and waited for her to tell me the story of an elderly man consumed with arthritis who'd died alone in a big old farmhouse in the middle of nowhere because his daughter had upped and left him to fend for himself. But she didn't. She said, 'he's left you the house. It's a mess so you'd better get over here before the end of summer if you want to sell it. I'm not sure the leak in the roof will last another stormy winter.'

Lewis wasn't surprised by my lack of emotion when I told him Bryn had passed away, nor the subsequent tears of relief once I realised what it meant: that I was finally free of the man I detested.

The invisible cord that bound us together through genetic history severed, at last.

Lewis tried to persuade me not to visit the place that had once been my childhood home, convinced it would upset me, but something drew me back. To gain closure?

I gathered up a box labelled *Carys* and kicked it along the dusty floor to where Lewis stood shaking his head. 'I can't carry any more than what I've got in my arms already.'

I stepped over the box and swiped him in jest. 'Wimp.'

He laughed lightly and swung round hitting his head on the low strung lightbulb.

Iefan called down the stairs. My son had been in the attic, smoking no doubt. He thought I couldn't smell it, but my nose was attuned to deceit. The lies were as thick in that house as the mildew covered walls that caused the paint to peel and the blackened windows to stick shut. The mould spores were seeping into Rhys' lungs. And I noticed he was already wheezing.

He'd suffered asthma since he was a small child. It was under control with Ventolin steroid inhalers, but after just an hour inside the damp farmhouse he'd already begun to sneeze and when he pelted down the steps into the cold dank basement after vacating the attic to allow his brother to smoke a cigarette, I noticed his eyes were watering and his nose was running. The dust mites weren't helping either.

I swallowed hard and pasted on a faux smile. The one nobody but Lewis recognised as a sign that being there was bringing it all back; the memory of leaving the house I'd shared with my parents, at sixteen years old and pregnant with Iefan.

'It's got potential,' said Lewis.

Yes, I thought. The potential to cost far more resources than I'd estimated.

I surveyed the room but could not imagine my younger self living there. Sadness and desolation rebounded off the walls. I needed the noise of traffic and busy streets. The city was my home now.

The farmhouse held so many awful memories it was hard to keep track of them all when I was stood in the epicentre, where my nightmares had begun.

I shoved things aside with my foot, glad the only items I'd found belonging to me were housed inside the box Lewis carried up the stairs while he traipsed after Iefan and Rhys.

I turned then, and a sharp pain shot down my back, sciatica and scoliosis- curvature of the spine and a damaged coccyx. My small frame had been unable to cope with the eight-pound child I'd birthed in a Bristol hospital barely of legal age.

I steadied myself by reaching for a box as I lunged forward, gripping hold of a sheet covering a large framed painting. It looked antique, though I'd never heard of the artist and had no idea what it might have been worth because money didn't interest me at all. All I'd ever wanted was to feel safe, loved. And I did now. Motherhood and wifedom had given me the affection my inner child had always craved.

As my eyes left the oil painting of the North border of Gwent Valleys, the mountainous hills stood sentry above the River Usk, I spotted, again, the stained mattress in my peripheral vision and without warning a flashback hit me square in the face.

A clinically steel grey room. A bright light splintering the darkness, shining unforgivably in my face. A tall, male figure in shadow.

The image disintegrated like dust. I was bent double, Lewis was moving toward me, holding out a hand to reach for mine so I could grab hold of him and hoist myself back into a standing position to walk off the pain that spread down the left-hand side of my spine and into my tingling leg just past the knee. Sometimes it worked to alleviate the pressure of my wonky spine on my sciatic nerve, but mostly it didn't.

'Come on, let's head outside.'

He led me toward the stables that were packed from floor to ceiling with the detritus of farming: unusable riding equipment, stacks of breeding ledgers and long-ago paid veterinary bills written in my father's own illegible scrawl.

The rain had begun while we were inside the dismal enclosed space that still wore the tang of manure. The smell clung to the brickwork and the supporting wooden beams that looked about ready to collapse above us.

'We'll clear out the house before we start on the outbuildings,' said Lewis, eyeing our stinking rotten surroundings.

I nodded in agreement.

I was soaked the moment I left the stable. The rain fell heavily and unsparingly, and I had to grip the compromised doorframe to prevent myself falling as my boots sunk and slid into puddles the colour of dark melted chocolate. I continued onward, despite the pain, and the difficulty caused by my stiff clothes sticking to my wet skin, and locked tight joints beneath my under-stretched muscles.

'Careful,' said Lewis.

I spun round, seeking firmer soil to find myself staring down at a pile of frayed clothes peeking out of the soggy earth. I lost my footing and reached out in time to grasp Lewis' arm, my fingers sliding down his raincoat and finding his ice-cold hand as I fell.

Lewis held me at the waist to stop me from landing in a position that would have left me bedridden, my back in agony for days, and hoisted me up. It was then that the sole of my shoe caught what I'd assumed was a torn green rag. I tried to kick it away as the soggy material clung to the leather, but it dragged along the pool of water that continued to flood the ground as it left a cylindrical piece of metal that I thought was a drainage pipe several meters from where I stood.

Lewis pulled at it and the filthy sodden fabric unravelled at my feet to display the tip of a cracked skull. 'A strange place to bury a sheep head.'

'I've never seen a lamb that small,' I winced as I knelt to retrieve the green cloth covering the rest of the bones.

'Don't,' he said, as my palms instinctively loosened their grip. 'It might be a device for satanic rituals.'

As I collected the offending item my eyes swept the ground, falling on the heaps of clay peat pushed forth by the force of the water that had sprung too abruptly through the soil, pumping out so fast it had created a river that ran toward the foundations of the house. 'That'll be where the damp's getting in.'

To my left I peered through the open doorway of the barn in search of an altar, goblet or dagger in the darkness, but there wasn't any evidence of voodoo. The barn was near empty. Which made my find more worrying.

My father had at one time collected stuffed animals brought to him by a friend who was a hobbyist in taxidermy. I wondered if the skull with a dent on its base belonged to a goat. Though how a once stuffed animal had ended up outside, I couldn't fathom.

I glanced back down at the item I held, fingers ice-cold and trembling. The shape of it . . .

I dropped it then, nausea rising from my stomach and into my throat making me heave. My face grew hot, my legs started to give way, and my shaking palms began to sweat.

The skull at my feet didn't belong to an animal. It was a child. A baby going by its size.

Lewis moved the green cloth aside with the toe of his shoe and we both gasped as several tiny bones fell from the fabric they had been disguised within. In the paddock, just beyond the garden of my father's house. Where he'd lived alone for the most part of two decades, my mother having died just weeks before my hasty departure with a child in my womb.

*Why is it here?*

That was a question I couldn't ask my father because his ashes were blown away by the wind over the Ebbw Vale Valley near the ancient ruins of a castle, according to Gwenda.

I stared at the skull, watching Lewis collect it from the deep water-logged ground where it had rolled and return it to the green cloth where he perched it on top of the rest of its mud-caked skeleton, piece by piece. He then folded the torn, dirty fabric back over the bones as they must have been when buried.

I watched him carry the covered skeleton into the barn, place it gently onto a dusty table beside a set of broken patio chairs and a worn King James bible.

Having disturbed the sinister object, I immediately backed away, consumed with dread.

*What the fuck have I unearthed?*

Human reason suggested the only logical explanation for burying an infant was if you were responsible in some way for his or her death.

I didn't know the man my father became, but what I remembered of him during my teenage years wasn't pleasant. He was cruel. But was he capable of something as abhorrent and heinous as murder?

Was it possible my father had more sins than I knew of?

I felt Lewis's arm over my shoulder, drawing me close to settle my nerves. 'We need to call the police.'

I nodded, unable to tear my eyes away from our find, shadowed by the walls of the barn.

# BRYN

*Brynmawr, Ebbw Vale, Wales, 1992*

Bryn Howell entered the farm, clumps of mud clung to his Wellingtons as he dusted off his jacket. Hay and feathergrass fell onto the mat. Rhiannon appeared in the doorway, the kitchen counter behind her gleaming. She held a cloth in her hand. Bryn noted the sour look on her face and watched as she folded her arms, the cloth leaving a damp stain on her chequered cotton shirt pressed tightly against her soft stomach. 'I thought you were going to be home hours ago.'

He opened his mouth to speak but she turned her back on him. 'Your dinner's cold,' she said, dumping the cloth on the counter and grabbing a plate from the draining board to wipe it dry with a towel.

Bryn often took off for a long walk after a tiring

day upstairs in his study. He especially liked it when the skies had cleared after a storm, when the fields smelt fresh and the wildlife hushed. But the unrelenting heat that summer made it impossible to climb the rugged countryside for long. Even after a decent amount of rainfall the air remained muggy.

'Where's Carys?'

'Out the back.'

His daughter had just turned ten. He turned and saw her through the open kitchen window as she rolled a wooden truck along the thick dry grass. The doll inside it tumbled out and she released an unheard squeal.

He stood beside the sink watching Carys brush a few stray strands of her thick rose blonde hair from her face, settling it behind her ear.

He liked to observe people when they weren't aware, but Carys was a knowing child. She looked up at him as if she felt his gaze through the glass. Always smiling, usually pleased to see her father. That day her features turned serious, eyes frozen on his before she turned, quickly gathered up her toys, and ran further down the uneven field, out of sight.

She climbed over the moss-covered stone wall to

where the sheep were grazing, which according to the land registry had been erected in 1715.

History was a funny thing he thought as he spun round to meet his wife's questioning face. The past could make or break a man. It shaped us. Our childhood was the one deciding factor on the person we would become.

Bryn's parents had put him in good stead for great things. He'd been taught to be independent. He didn't need friends. He'd joined the local accountancy firm at the tender age of fifteen and had met his wife only a couple of years later. But the cost of running an office in town quickly became a tedious money-snatcher so he'd shut up shop to run his business in the spare bedroom-turned-study, upstairs.

Bryn's father was a good, hard-working man. A steel miner. He rarely spoke unless it was to admonish him. His mother brought him and his two siblings up practically single-handedly. Spending most of her time on the farm.

Bryn's work ethic and perfectionist attitude were traits he'd developed as a child, inherited from his parents. He used to take care of his ungrateful jealous brothers when they were young. They were inseparable until he'd inherited his father's estate. Now they refused to speak to him.

Rhiannon nudged him, told him to sit, and he pulled out a chair to eat the lamb stew his wife had spent hours simmering in the stuffy kitchen. The meat was soft and tender, the carrots crunchy, the wild garlic lodged between his teeth.

'How is it?' said Rhiannon.

'Good. Thank you.'

He ate like a man starved after returning from a deployment to war, licked the spoon clean, then pushed his chair back and stood, dropping the bowl into the sink. He heard his wife tut as the spoon clanged, the handle lodging itself in the plughole as he turned toward the door.

He stopped, motioned to the window. 'I'm going into the barn,' he said, ignoring Rhiannon's sigh. 'The hens need feeding.'

'Go on then, but don't be long. *Only Fools and Horses* are on tonight and I don't want to miss it.'

Television was Rhiannon's vice. He had his own, although it wasn't something that he could disclose to anyone, least of all his wife. Rhiannon would consider it a sin.

He traipsed down the narrow path and forced the creaky door of the barn open. He stuffed his hand inside the bag of grain and tossed it haphazardly onto the ground. The hens clucked and scrabbled amongst the haybed, dipping their beaks into the oats and seeds and pecking at them hungrily. When one followed him to the door, expecting to be released of the confined space it was housed within, he nudged it back with his heavy boot and it scurried away.

The barn stank of soiled hay, the clumps of which stuck to the soles of his boots as he trod back out into the sun. He could see his daughters head bobbing up and down behind the wall. 'Carys?'

She stopped playing and dropped the toys from her spindly hands. Her rake-thin arms glowed in the sunlight as she stood and turned toward his deep gruff voice.

'Over here,' he pointed to the shovel and the sun-bleached plastic bucket that lay on the stiff dry grass at his feet.

She climbed the wall and walked slowly toward her father, bent at the waist to collect the bucket, struggled to drag the spade along the ground, and without a word, features set hard and impassive she obeyed his command.

Back inside the farm, he dumped his boots on the mat beside his Wellingtons, dropping flakes of mud onto the carpet and decorating the skirting board with strands of hay before entering the living room where Rhiannon had perched herself in front of the television with a pot of tea. There was a plate of biscuits on the tray beside an empty cup. He crammed one into his mouth, crumbs nestling inside his thick beard. She poured him a drink which he took from her trembling hand.

'You got another one of your migraines?'

'Yes.'

'Go and have a lie down upstairs. I'll call Carys in when she's done with the mucking out.'

Rhiannon stood, holding one hand across her right eye so she could see straight and walked painfully slowly from the room.

He gave it five minutes before he put his boots on and exited the back door. He walked round to the side of the house where Carys stood waiting for permission to leave the barn.

'All done?'

She nodded, dropping the spade to hoist the

bucket up to empty out onto the waste pile.

'Follow me,' he said then, leading her into the potting shed and closing the door behind them.

She looked up at him with haunted eyes. Her eyelashes fluttering as she blinked.

He pulled the empty chocolate wrapper from the pocket of his jeans and dangled it in front of her. 'I found this in the barn.'

He noticed a nervous twitch above her left temple and waited for her to tell him it wasn't her, that she hadn't been so impatient she couldn't wait for supper. That she hadn't gone into the snack cupboard above the range and taken it.

'I didn't steal it.'

'You know lying is a sin, right?'

She nodded once, opened her mouth to form an excuse, thought better of it, closed it again like a goldfish then surprised him and said, 'I was hungry.'

He smiled, lent over her, his nose barely an inch from her face, his breath stroking her lips. 'Then you will learn the value of food. When I was a boy, I was lucky enough to get scraps for dinner. There were three of us, and we never complained. And we certainly daren't consider stealing from our parents.'

'Mother said I could have it.'

He felt his blood pressure rise. 'You're a liar,' he spat.

'I'm not,' she said, face screwed up in defiance, stomping one foot onto the dirty wooden floor.

'You know what they do to children who steal in some Eastern countries?'

She swallowed hard and he could only imagine the images she was conjuring as he narrowed his eyes and dropped his voice. 'They cut off their thieving little hands.'

She gasped and jolted back as he reached for the saw.

'Come here.'

'No,' she cried, pushing herself up against the wall of the shed.

Her eyes in the near darkness were glistening with fear, pupils dilated, her hair sticking to her forehead from the heat. Or was it the sweat of fear?

He lunged for her and dragged her by an arm to the countertop, sunlit from the bright rays emanating through the gaps in the slatted wooden door.

She tried to tug her arm free, but he was stronger than her, so it was futile.

He gripped her wrist tight and slammed her hand down onto the countertop, pressing the full weight of his elbow on her fingers to hold her still. She winced and fought, punching his forearm with her free hand and kicking his shin, so he pressed harder until she wailed.

He threw his arm back, wielding the saw before slamming it down hard on the countertop inches from her thumb so that it stuck in the plywood.

She screamed and hot tears slid down her panicked face.

He released her and she fell onto the hard floor. He smiled down at her, satisfied she'd learnt her lesson. 'Get up and go straight to your room. You're not to leave it until the morning.'

'But what if I need the toilet?' she sobbed.

'Then you can piss yourself.'

A moment of understanding passed between them. The consequence of bedwetting was far worse than a couple of sore fingers.

She stood on quivering legs.

'Beat it.'

She turned, shoved open the door and ran out into the warm July sun, sniffling as she headed for the house.

He closed the door of the shed, holding Carys in sight as he followed her inside.

# CARYS

*Brynmawr, Ebbw Vale, Wales, 2018*

The headlights of the police car glared through the half open curtains.

Lewis opened the door before they knocked.

The boys were upstairs. Iefan stood at the top of the staircase, holding his mobile phone above his head trying to get a signal, and making ghostly noises while Rhys looked up at him from the passageway, unperturbed.

Lewis invited in two plain clothed detectives.

'Detective Inspector Locke,' the thirty-something-year-old woman said, showing me her ID card. 'Blaenau Gwent Police.' She nodded to her colleague and introduced me to Detective Sergeant Jones.

She smiled wanly at Lewis, followed us into the living room, then baulked slightly at the stuffed owl perched on the bookcase, thankfully the only one of my father's friends' projects still dwelling on the property.

Goosebumps covered my flesh when I looked at it, so I avoided it's stare and settled back onto the sofa.

'We received a call from an operator about some bones?'

'Yes, in the barn. It's a . . . baby,' I choked out the words.

Lewis motioned for DS Jones to follow him out the door, leading the male detective across the sodden ground and into the barn to view the evidence.

Thick clouds filled the dusky sky that loomed over the farm.

'Is this your house?' said DI Locke.

I turned away from the window to face the eagle-eyed detective. 'No, my father's.'

'Is he around to speak to?' she said, pulling a mobile phone out of her coat, which she appeared to be intending to make notes on.

'He's dead.'

She barely took her eyes off me as she began to type.

I swallowed the bile that threatened to leap from

my throat, noting that her body language silently requested further explanation.

'We weren't close. He passed away four months ago. A neighbour of his, Gwenda, found my number on my website – I'm a photographer – and called to inform me that he'd died. She knew where he kept his will because he'd employed her as his home-help, and he'd left her some money for taking care of him. She dealt with the funeral and the solicitor. He left me the farm.'

'I see.' She didn't bother to ask if I'd attended the funeral, which I had not. She studied me for a moment then said, 'did you touch the remains?'

'Yes, I . . . did. My husband too.'

'Our forensics team will examine the bones, so we'll have to eliminate the transference of your DNA from them. It's unlikely, considering the weather and the state of them – according to your report – that your prints will be on them, but as a precaution I need to arrange for you to come down to the station, so we can take your fingerprints etc.'

'Yes, of course.'

'Have you got anywhere to stay?'

'The Premier Inn. We, uh . . . we travelled from

Bristol to clear the place out, to put it on the market. We had no intention of staying here.'

If she noticed my accented *here*, she said nothing to suggest it, though she clearly recognised my south western lilt because she sounded Bristolian herself.

'Which area of Bristol are you from?' she said.

'Redland.'

She pressed her lips together and forced a tight smile. I knew what she thought, that we were old money. Just because my father owned a plot of land in the countryside it didn't mean we were snobs. To prove it I offered to make her tea, making sure she followed me into the grimy kitchen to see exactly how the other half lived.

She stared at the seat I pulled away from the messy dining table after I'd knocked a pile of bills and receipts from the chair, leaving them to cascade onto the floor into a small hill of paper. 'I'll stand,' she said. 'Do you have coffee?'

'Sure.' I busied myself, boiling the kettle, rooting through the cupboards for a cup, deciding to wash out the camping mug I'd brought in from the car, realising there was no milk, offering to pour her some luke-warm coffee from the thermos, and handing it to her with a tremor.

I didn't ask her what I wanted to, because I wasn't sure I would have liked the answer she might have theorised: why were the remains of a baby wrapped up in some cloth buried on the land of my father's house?

DS Jones scrambled up the narrow path, through the front door, and tread hastily down the passageway into the living room, finding me and DI Locke seated on the sofa. He looked to his colleague, his brow creased in thought, and said, 'baby bones, alright.' Then he turned to my husband and said, 'I'm going to call a Crime Scene Investigation unit to come and collect them. Unfortunately, that makes the entire property a crime scene. I'm afraid you're not going to be able to re-enter the premises until we've established that they're the only ones.'

'You think . . . there could be more?'

DS Jones turned to me then. 'We have to obtain a warrant to search the land as well as the building as a precaution.'

I nodded, suddenly feeling dizzy, my stomach churning. 'What will you do once you've finished examining them? Will they be buried?'

Goosebumps crawled along my neckline as I thought about how we'd disturbed the gravesite. I imagined my mother watching me from the chair parked in front of the corner unit where a photograph of her stood as erect as she appeared in the picture. I drew the bones from the ground. If anyone were to be damned to hell for all eternity it would be me.

I shut down my mother's religious influence the moment I recognised her voice attempting to interrupt DI Locke's reply. 'We have a team of specialists who will determine approximately how old they are and estimate who they might belong to. But it's going to take some time.' Insinuating she had no idea when the infant could be laid to rest, properly, as he or she should have been long ago.

'We'll have to analyse the dress too, to determine if it belongs to the mother,' said DS Jones.

Dress?

My pulse quickened.

The cloth the bones were wrapped up in was green.

Seren Lloyd was wearing an emerald green dress the day she disappeared.

*The bones belong to a baby Carys, not a twelve-*

*year-old girl.*

'It must have been a frightening discovery for you,' said DS Jones. *'I've* not come across anything like it before.'

DI Locke moved swiftly toward the door with her mobile phone pressed to her ear. She stood out in the cold for several minutes talking to 'DCS Evans,' leaving the front door open, allowing the damp air to seep down the passageway and soak through my jumper, turning my limbs to ice.

When she returned, we waited, the six of us, in the living room. Perched on the sofa or stood against the wall staring into space for over twenty minutes before another set of headlights pierced through the night and flashed between the gaps in the burnt meringue coloured, threadbare curtains.

'The boys in whites are here,' said DI Locke, moving toward the door. I assumed she meant CSI.

I scooted past four men and women wearing nylon all-in-ones, coverlets over their shoes, and masks over their faces, carrying cameras, video recorders, and large see-through snap-bags.

Lewis ushered the kids into the car while I handed the keys of the property to DI Locke who stared at me intently. 'We'll call you when we're done. It's likely to take a day or two, depending on how it works out. Your mobile number was logged with the call handler, so I'll give you a ring on that and let you know how we're getting on. And I'll be in touch about the swabs we'll need to take from you.' She must have seen the confusion written across my face because she added, 'it's a giant cotton bud. One of the team will run it along the inside of your cheek to collect a sample of your DNA, like we discussed.'

'Oh, yes. Of course.'

I headed for the car, not bothering to look back at the house or her. Dread gripping hold of my chest and squeezing it tight like an elastic band had been pulled taut around my ribs.

I envisioned the skull then. The hole above the forehead plate where the fontanel hadn't had time to conjoin. The dent at the base and wondering if the fracture was what caused the infant's death.

The baby was less than a month old going by the size of it. Someone was missing a new-born, and all that time it had been there, lying in the dirt, fifty yards from my father's house.

In the car, on the drive back to the hotel we'd

already booked reservations for I managed to get enough signal to search the local online news for the report of a missing baby or the disappearance of a pregnant woman in the area, but nothing filled the screen. Then I thought about the emerald green dress.

Seren Lloyd disappeared twenty-four years ago. The internet was in its infancy then. There were no online articles available relating to the case, except for an update from a retired detective Murrow of Gwent County Police during a cold case review that had delivered nothing in 2012.

I shared the half-page news-piece with myself via Facebook Messenger as Lewis pulled the car into the forecourt of the Premier Inn and determined to finish my investigation the following morning.

On our drive to west from our home in Bristol I could not have foreseen our visit to Ebbw Vale (The Valley of The Wild Horse) would force us to put the despatching of my father's crap back due to such an awful discovery. Travelling out of smoggy Redland, surrounded by urban architecture, people, and noise to the rolling hills and steep inclines of the rocky heather-coated mountainside was meant to be a novel experience for the boys who'd never visited Wales. But right then, in the car, on that dark dreary night all I wanted to do was return home to my safe, ignorant, ordinary life.

Seren's face was frozen on the touchscreen of my mobile phone. I swiped at the image, but it wouldn't fade- my Android suffering from ghost screen.

I doubted the townsfolk had ever ceased believing she would be found.

My mother was heartbroken when she heard the news. Everyone was distraught regardless of whether they were parents or not because it had happened in a sleepy tight-knit town with a low crime rate.

It seemed to affect my mother, Rhiannon, more because I was the same age as Seren when she disappeared, and an only child too.

'Don't go further than the track, Carys. And don't speak to any strangers,' she warned my twelve-year-old self.

If I saw a car approach the roadside at the end of the lane while I ambled through the conjoining fields, I dropped whatever I was doing and ran from the surrounding land and back into the apparent safety of the farm.

These days we know better of course. Rarely does a stranger snatch a child they've never met from the street. They're usually taken by adults who know them well. Often someone especially close to them, such as a family member, friend, neighbour, or teacher. Mostly the person responsible for a missing child is one of their own parents. But in the nineties people wore blinkers. It couldn't happen to them or their daughter, until it did.

I'd thought about Seren in the twenty-four years since she vanished, but leaving the area helped to blur the memory. Yet from the moment I felt the fragile skull in the palms of my hands I became infected with sorrow and once I learned the fabric the infant's remains were held together within was a green dress, I couldn't seem to rid the awful images that scrambled around inside my head.

Something stirred inside me, uncoiled, and the flashbulb of a memory temporarily blinded me.

My mother perched on the edge of her chair, staring at the photograph of Seren displayed to fill the television screen, as the reporter disclosed her last known movements. Tears pooled in her eyes.

My father entered the room, took one look at the

television, and his face stilled.

'I can't imagine anything like that happening to our girl,' said my mother, almost forgetting I was stood beside her.

She usually kept her thoughts and feelings locked up inside her. But something had disturbed the equilibrium. My mother, typically detached, showed concern that the girl had gone and relief that it hadn't been me taken from the roadside.

My father slipped off his jacket, ignoring her worry, exited the living room and trod into the kitchen, where I found him staring through the window at the sunburnt grass. His face emotionless, contradicting his physical turmoil. Shoulders tense, arms trembling, and knuckles white as he gripped the edge of the countertop. His gaze directed somewhere past the hen-filled barn.

Was he staring at the sky or the ground where a mound of freshly dug peat had stirred the earth?

# BRYN

*Brynmawr, Ebbw Vale, Wales, 1994*

The blazing sun shone down on the valley where Bryn steadied himself on a clump of rock as he stood gazing at the horizon before him.

His ancestors had trundled along the same route on horseback many moons ago. The area hummed with history: the ghosts of battle-fallen soldiers after a bomb had hit the earth, the dead men trapped beneath the surface of the old shaft after the mine's collapse, leaving the soil as black as ash. His mother and father, their faces slick with sweat and dirty from working the farm, the place he called home. An inheritance he couldn't have been prouder of.

He turned his attention to his daughter.

Carys' skin was bronzed from the sun. Her thick wavy hair, like her mothers, fell to her shoulders and ended just above her chest. She was growing too fast. He didn't like it one bit.

Rhiannon's footsteps fell softly against the crabgrass and itchy nettles as she wound her way across the fell and up to the peak with a view of sugar-loaf mountain: a smudge of blue-grey in the distance. 'It's beautiful here, Bryn.'

'It is that.'

They stood awhile, in silence. Breathing in the scent of wildflowers. Content.

But the calm didn't last long.

They returned to the farm to the sound of sirens in the near distance.

Bryn's grip on the door handle, unbeknownst to his wife or daughter, tightened as he shut out the world behind them. But he couldn't escape the news.

It was on the local television channel first. Then later, the radio, as he drove his car to the petrol station to valet using the car wash and wax. And in his wife's eyes as she sat limp watching the update on the six o'clock news that evening when he returned home.

Seren Lloyd was missing. Had last been seen walking home from school by Glynis Owens, the owner of the grocery shop on the corner of Castle Lane. She was heading to her dance practice for Eisteddfod but hadn't arrived home at 4:45pm as her waiting mother had expected. Her teacher, Gareth Price, was assisting the police with their enquiries.

Bryn's fingers found the remote control and his thumb dug into the *off* button. The television screen went blank.

Rhiannon tutted. 'I was watching that.'

'It won't help, you know.'

'No, you're right,' she said, standing to attention like a soldier about to go into battle. She marched from the room, tugged her coat from the hooked stand beside the front door and flung it over her shoulders.

'Where are you going?'

'The police are setting up a search party. I'm going to go and look for her.'

'It's dark and cold.'

'Then I'll take a scarf and a torch.'

'Don't go, Rhiannon. What good will it do you getting all worked up? You'll end up with another migraine.'

She ignored him and pulled open the front door.

'Think about this for a minute,' he said, placing his solid hands on her shoulders. 'Carys needs you here.'

She turned, a frown lining her forehead. 'She's asleep.'

As she stepped outside, his hands slipped from her body like a weight being lifted. She breathed in the cool night-time air and said, 'if that was Carys out there on her own in the dark I'd want everyone out looking for her.'

Bryn closed the door on his wife's retreating form and stopped at the bottom of the staircase before entering the living room, looking up at his tired looking daughter stood at the top.

'What's happened? Where's mother gone?' said Carys.

'Go back to bed.'

'I heard her say my name.'

He narrowed his eyes and said, 'your mother was asking if I knew where you were this afternoon. She couldn't understand why you were late home.'

'What did you tell her?' she said, rubbing her sleepy eyes, her voice rising in concern.

'I told her you were with me. That we were having some father and daughter time.'

He saw her throat incline as she swallowed hard and bit her lip, hands instinctively reaching for her arms, crossed over her flat, bare stomach. A self-preservation tactic. A defence mechanism.

'Go to bed. I'll be up in a minute to tuck you in.'

She spun round fast and jogged back to her room, slamming the door shut in haste.

He heard the lock slide into place. He rolled his eyes. That wouldn't stop him from entering, but it might slow him down.

# CARYS

*Brynmawr, Ebbw Vale, Wales, 2018*

The Premier Inn was situated five miles from Blaen-Afon Road. Past the primary school Seren had gone to, Asda, Halfords, the Market Hall cinema, and the golf club where my father used to play before he developed angina. An ATS garage, the Kingdom Hall my mother used to attempt to lure strangers into and convince them to become Jehovah's Witnesses, and McDonald's where we bought burgers, fries, and cola to stuff our faces and slurp down before entering the hotel.

The village hall was to our left where the Women's Institute held their fortnightly meetings to bake cakes, knit clothes for the underprivileged, and swap reviews for their latest book club read according to the leaflet in the entranceway. To our right was the hospice with a view of the wildlife reserve my father refused to accept a bed to reside in, said the petite receptionist who greeted us in the hotel lobby and immediately recognised our names.

'Gwenda works here. She does the phones on Sunday when it's quiet.'

Was there nothing that woman did, and nobody she knew?

What was more concerning, was that she'd already been gossiping about us to the locals. What had she told them about our discovery, where a reel of blue and white tape danced in the breeze around the four acres of land owned by my father? The press was already snapping photographs from the police cordon at the end of the lane wondering why the CSI's were digging the garden up.

The population wasn't exactly small for a town experiencing *restructuring*. But I hadn't expected it to still be so confined that Gwenda had begun her own reporting of recent events to local busybodies.

I ignored the nosy old bat behind the counter, took our key cards, one each for me and Lewis, and left Iefan and Rhys outside the door to their room before walking upstairs to our double bedroom on the first floor. It was after all an unplanned holiday. One I'd already begun to regret. I didn't like the thought of us sleeping on separate floor levels, so insisted the boys send me a text message before they crawled into bed, whatever time that would be, and reminded them we would meet in the restaurant at 8:00am the following morning.

I slipped off my shoes and undressed the moment I entered the room walking a few paces behind Lewis. The familiar purple décor associated with the Premier Inns I'd stayed in previously had been replaced with steel grey. Muted, but smart.

Lewis pulled me toward him before I could reach for my bed T-shirt and shorts. He smoothed down my hair and kissed me. I sighed, resting my head against his solid chest. 'I know this thing at your dads has put a spin on our plans but it's Sunday tomorrow. Maybe we should take a walk around the place before buying a roast lunch in that Brewers Fayre we passed.'

The last thing I wanted to do was wander the streets of the place I couldn't wait to leave twenty years ago. I'd read an article online that a flower garden had been planted where the former steelworks site had been. Lewis had mentioned visiting the place several times in the days leading up to our departure, but I kept brushing him off. I knew the conversation was going to return to the same topic if I didn't immediately snap the subject shut.

'Why don't we head into Newport and have a look around Friars Walk shopping centre instead?'

The town where I spent none of my youth was only twenty-three miles south east of where we were staying. Nowhere near the Brecon Beacons my father insisted we visit one weekend for some local sight-seeing. Or the Abertillery Museum I apparently puked up in after spending too long in a hot stuffy coach for a school trip after the driver got lost. And miles away from the B-road where I'd hitched a lift to the Blaenavon ironworks the first time I ran away.

'Okay. Whatever you want.'

Sometimes I wished Lewis would make the decisions in our marriage. It was tiring holding the fort all the time.

I looked up at him and grazed his cheek with my lips, inhaling his aftershave, before pushing him back on the bed and straddling him, unbuttoning his shirt and lifting it up and over his head.

His muscular torso was coated in fine dark hairs.

His rugby player physique gave the impression he regularly worked out, but there was no need. He was naturally built like a bodyguard.

*Nothing like your father*, said a little voice in the back of my head.

'You okay?' said Lewis, face etched with concern.

'Yeah, fine.'

'Can you release me then?' He glanced down at my hands pressed down hard on his wrists as though to prevent him from touching me.

'S . . . sorry.'

'It's fine. As long as you're not about to start getting into all that handcuffs and whips malarkey like the characters in those novels you women enjoy reading these days.'

'No.'

He laughed nervously as I prised my nails from his skin, leaving half-moon indents in his flesh.

'Don't look so worried. You know I don't mind a bit of slap and tickle, I'm just not into the whole . . . What did I say?'

'Nothing,' I said, leaving the bed, not wanting him to see my ghostly pale face, lips tight with a hatred burning through my veins, a rage I'd never felt before.

My hands trembled, and my legs moved robotically into the bathroom where I shut the door and crouched onto the linoleum, resting my spine against the solid wood.

What's my fathers body got to do with my husbands?

'You're being dramatic as usual,' said my mother from the corner of the room.

Though I knew my mother wasn't there the room tilted on its axis and I felt myself being drawn to the past, to a conversation I'd almost forgotten we'd shared.

'Drama queen,' she said.

I faintly heard my reply. 'I'm telling you, she was abducted.'

'It's starting to look that way yes, but we can't be sure that's what happened to Seren.'

'I saw her.'

My mother stormed toward me. She towered over me and snarled. 'Whatever you think you know, you must keep it to yourself. Gossips around here, the lot of them.'

'But I'm telling the truth. Why won't anyone believe me?'

'Because you're a compulsive liar, Carys. Nobody's going to listen to the storyteller girl who cries wolf any time things aren't going her way. You're just inventing a reason not to go to school based on the sad fact that a child is missing. It's sacrilegious.'

'She got into a blue car.'

My mother's eyes narrowed, and her face contorted with irritation as she realised the significance of what I'd said.

'What are you trying to get at, Carys?'

'I'm not *getting at* anything.'

She shook her head and turned away. 'Fantasist.' But she stalled, as though an invisible forcefield was preventing her from leaving the room. She hovered in the doorway. 'Besides, she was heading for her dance class with Mr Price. The school is at least a quarter of a mile from yours so if you *did* see her being forced into someone's car you would have been in the wrong area.' Then I heard, 'which means you're in trouble,' but I thought that might have been my inner monologue getting its own word in.

My mouth hung open. I heard a loud thudding as Lewis' fist connected to the door. My spine vibrated against the shuddering wood. He knocked again, the sound reminding me of a vehicle door slamming.

I could see the car as clearly now as I had then, as if I was once again stood on the pavement opposite the turning to Castle Lane, about ten yards from the grocery shop where Glynis Owens used to work.

A light blue vehicle. I remembered the car, because the make and model had been recalled for having a defective central locking mechanism that meant the keys for every car sold in the same shade of blue worked to open, lock, and start all the others. The first I'd heard of it was from an episode of Watchdog. My father threw his empty teacup at the television in rage. 'That's why the little fuckers stole it. They knew Rhiannon. It's on the bastard programme.'

'What is?' cried mother.

'The lads that Mrs Edwards claims she saw taking my car for a joyful ride. They must have known they didn't need to hotwire it.'

He explained the manufacturing problem to my mother, and she exhaled a long-held breath. 'Every cloud, Bryn.'

My father rose from his chair, face red and hot, fists clenched at his sides, his entire body shaking with a temper I don't recall witnessing as strong emanating from him before that day.

She spoke softly to pacify him. 'It was bound to happen one day with all the thieving little sods round here. It could even have been taken accidentally by someone who owns the same car. The fact it's gone now means that rust-bucket is not your problem anymore. You've been saying you wanted a new vehicle for ages. The insurance will buy you a new, better car.'

He stepped back and relaxed. 'You're right.'

'Good riddance to it, I say.'

'Yes,' he said. He turned to me to receive a nod of approval that he was right, as always, but I pretended I hadn't heard, creeping away from the room that held so much venom I could almost feel it layering itself upon my skin.

'Carys?' he said.

*

'Carys? Are you okay in there?' Lewis' concerned voice rose an octave in impatience.

I scrambled up from the hard linoleum and opened the bathroom door. 'Sorry, I . . .'

Lewis took my hands in his and led me into the hotel bedroom.

'Why'd you freak out?'

I took a deep breath intending to tell him about Seren Lloyd, the emerald green dress she was wearing when she disappeared, that I saw her minutes before she reportedly went missing getting into a car the same colour, make, and model as my father's. That I didn't know why, but the moment I glanced down at his bare chest, I thought I remembered my father's naked torso, which I would have because he spent a lot of time in the sun-drenched fields of the farm wearing nothing but shorts and steel toe-capped boots. Though for some reason, I couldn't explain, I felt unease over the image. As if the memory had been distorted with age, with experience.

I heard Iefan at the door, calling through the thick wood, telling me that I'd left my mobile phone in the car.

Lewis opened it for me, noting my arms clamped across my waist.

'It's ringing, and it's set the alarm off. The receptionist is going nuts trying to find the owner of the car to inform them, but I don't think you signed it in did you?'

'No,' said Lewis. 'They usually request your registration for legal purposes or fire regulations or something...'

They were both staring at me. I must have looked as shell-shocked as I felt.

'Mum are you okay?' said Iefan.

'Yes, honey. I'm fine. I thought they only needed CCTV footage these days.'

Lewis raised his eyebrows at my fast turnaround, at my change of subject. 'Really. I'm okay. Just feeling tired and overwhelmed, I guess.'

'Sure,' they spoke together, their disbelief evident.

I didn't need to ask Iefan why he was outside, or how he knew my mobile phone was the cause of the car alarm going off, because I could smell cigarette smoke on him, and the ashtray was right where we'd parked. It wouldn't have surprised me if he'd clipped the wing mirror in his rush to return to his room and set it off himself.

I waited until Lewis had grabbed the keys from his jacket pocket and had left the room to collect my phone and reset the alarm before I pulled Iefan aside and said, 'you don't need to keep secrets from me. You're old enough to smoke. Not that I agree with you doing it.'

'I know,' his shoulders drooped. 'I was protecting you.'

'From what?'

'I didn't think you'd want to discover your eldest son smoking just a few months after finding out your dad had died of a coronary.'

Iefan's was a sensitive soul. Thoughtful and caring. Introverted. He'd have taken the time to consider whether to tell me, his analytical brain working overtime to decide not to. I smiled and thanked him for his honesty. 'Better late than never.'

I couldn't blame him. Perhaps he was beginning to realise he should have taken our advice, listened to our life lessons, practiced what we preach because mine and Lewis' experience came from making the same mistakes. But I thought if I pushed Iefan too hard, the pressure might propel him away. I wanted my kids to feel as though they could talk to me about anything. Something I didn't feel able to do with mine. If Iefan wanted to smoke, he was old enough to learn how unpleasant it was without me helicoptering him out of it.

I hadn't smoked in years, and rarely drank. I'd started smoking when my mother fell ill and realised, I might end up living alone in the house with my father.

I felt suffocated beneath his watchful gaze. He wasn't overprotective, his hold over me was more akin to control. I was nothing but a possession to Bryn.

He liked to show me off as though I was a trophy on his arm but became jealous if anyone paid me any attention, especially men. He couldn't stand the thought of his little girl being anyone else's but his. That's why I had to escape.

# RHIANNON

*Brynmawr, Ebbw Vale, Wales, 1996*

It had been two years since Seren Lloyd had gone missing. Two years since the community first felt the nagging suspicion and fear, the uncertainty and crushing realisation that someone with a good knowledge of the local area must have had something to do with her disappearance. Which meant whoever had taken her was most likely still around. The devil living amongst them.

Her loss was a regular topic of gossip amongst the pensioners fitness class Rhiannon passed on the green as she walked to work. She couldn't escape it. Neither did she want to. A small part of her was curious, wanted to delve into the intricacies of the case, investigate what motive had led someone to want to take a young girl away from her family.

Had she been kidnapped because her parents owed someone money? Had she run away from an abusive household? Had she been snatched by a predatory neighbour? Or abducted by a woman desperate for a child of her own?

The entire town looked at everyone as if they were a suspect. Had he taken her? Had she?

Her own suspicions began that summer, when weeks had passed and still the police flooded the town. When after months of knocking on doors to speak to people, checking bins and outhouses, distributing posters, requesting information via CrimeStoppers, and trekking through fields, forestry, streams, and down lanes there was still no sign of her. When a second year passed and any hope of finding Seren alive had all but vanished into the ether, along with the probability her body would be discovered, something gnawed at Rhiannon.

She'd asked Bryn to search for Seren with her, but he always excused his lack of interest with the missing girl by claiming a busy work schedule, tiredness, or inventing the sudden need to 'get on with some household maintenance' which had before then never been mentioned. 'It needs doing,

Rhiannon,' was his favourite saying. Along with, 'how would you cope without a man about the house?' She never knew if it was a threat that she might one day wake up without him, or if he secretly desired a life apart from her.

Bryn had always been a serious man. He spent far too much time wandering the area surrounding their home alone. Which was why she always asked him, 'have you seen anything?' Meaning a piece of clothing sticking out of the reeds along the riverbank, a discarded shoe in the road, or a child that looked like Seren with an adult who wasn't supposed to be with her walking through the town. But he always came up empty. 'No, Rhiannon. I haven't.'

'You could look harder.'

He'd give her a look that said, 'watch your mouth,' and she did. Not because she was afraid of him. But because she feared God's disapproval if she bit back at the man whom she'd devoted twenty years of her life to, had promised to love, honour, and obey.

He liked to walk, for hours sometimes. He often took Carys with him. He doted on his daughter, went out of his way to teach her to become a strong capable young woman. And to achieve that goal, at the detriment of his marriage, he sometimes did things Rhiannon didn't agree with.

He disciplined Carys like an army sergeant, but in time her daughter stopped lying and trying to get her own way, and became a well-behaved, good mannered child. The problem was, she'd recently become withdrawn. Bryn was strict. Insisting she didn't leave the house to play on the street with her friends, couldn't attend sleepovers, and gave her a curfew so she wouldn't stay out late at parties. He didn't trust boys, so he ensured if they were present at a birthday celebration to park out of sight and hang around to ensure she was safe. He even drove the car right up to the front of the house half an hour before he expected her to walk out the front door. He was her own personal security-guard.

But the night she arrived home red eyed, her hair sticking to her face, damp with tears, embarrassed to find her father waiting outside to collect her- far too early, she hadn't been pleased and he'd given her what for. The incident left her feeling guilty and Rhiannon questioned if they were too strict on her, would it push Carys away?

Thereafter she insisted – begged and pleaded –

her husband to allow Carys to travel with a friend to Cardiff by bus, unescorted. The daytrip went well, so the following weekend he'd delivered her to Zoe's party (something she didn't agree with but allowed thinking if she didn't Carys would hate her more). Besides, she wasn't in charge. That was Bryn's job. Though she never worded it, that was how it was supposed to be.

Bryn collected Carys fifteen minutes early from Zoe's fourteenth birthday party because he'd caught her on the doorstep 'eating the face off Zoe's brother.'

Rhiannon thought grounding a fitting punishment for a teenage girl. She was too old for Bryn's prior use of discipline. And she'd never been comfortable with him doing it in the first place. They'd argued countless times about it in the past, but her disagreement was futile. Once Bryn had decided to do something, nobody could stop him. He was a loose cannon when he was mad.

But since Seren's disappearance, his anger had abated, and he seemed determined not to allow anything to happen to his precious girl.

Carys seemed to always be at his side. It didn't bother Rhiannon until she realised the fractured relationship that she shared with her daughter might have been caused by Bryn's over-protective behaviour and not the reason for it.

Rhiannon blamed herself: the migraines forcing her to the bedroom where she often remained for days, nauseous, dizzy, shaking, and unable to think coherently, least of all have a conversation with her family at the dinner table. This pushed Bryn and Carys together. But once Rhiannon discovered the reason for her blurred vision and received a diagnosis for the catatonic states she was often left in, it was too late to make up for those lost years and rekindle her floundering relationship with Carys.

Rhiannon relinquished her tight grip on the newspaper and smoothed down the pages, returning her mind to the facts, and picking at them from her bed, as she did these days, with nothing much else to do to satisfy the boredom of staring at the same four walls, tired, her muscles too weak to stand.

The contemporary dance schoolteacher, Gareth Price, had returned home to his girlfriend within hours of speaking to the police. He was not questioned further. His alibi and several witnesses took care of that. Glynis Owens, the shopkeeper, had explained how Seren appeared 'happy' and 'carefree' when she passed the grocers at approximately 3:15pm; ten minutes after leaving her best friend in the playground of the secondary to walk the short distance to the dance school.

The day Seren disappeared Bryn's vehicle was being stolen from the front of the house. He didn't report the car missing until the next day, viewing it as 'an obstruction to police search and rescue resources.' But thanks to Mrs Edwards' recognition of it, the two lads who'd stolen the vehicle were brought into custody for theft and released on bail when they'd admitted taking the car and setting fire to it eleven miles away in Pontypool. They lost their licences, were each given twelve months suspended sentences, and fined five hundred pounds.

How Bryn hadn't seen the vehicle being taken as he worked from his desk in his study upstairs, hadn't concerned the police. The timeline he gave Rhiannon didn't quite match the one Bryn gave to them. But the car was in such a state the police couldn't garner any DNA from it to prove what the lads had done with it before they had been caught.

The police suspected the vehicle had been used for

a burglary they couldn't prove had occurred unless someone reported it. The vehicle was held in an impound for a month then crushed. Nobody had yet figured out what had happened to Seren or who had taken her. And Carys hadn't mentioned the blue car to anyone after her father had dealt with her.

But Rhiannon had thought it strange – though she daren't question Bryn's motive – when he'd asked the police to give the two thieving lads some leeway. 'There's far more important crimes going on right now, huh?'

At the time she wasn't surprised by his outward display of concern for the missing girl. She had married Bryn Howell because of his charming personality, the affection he gave her, and his ability to stand up for her, to present a united front. Something he'd shown a lot that year when people whispered horrible things about her in the street. But when the search died down, she wondered if his sympathy was a show, an act he used to express his insincere worry only when in the presence of others. And her guarded observation of him intensified over the next twenty-four months. Because Bryn, typically quick-tempered was unusually calm after his precious car was stolen, and he appeared distracted in the days following the theft.

Rhiannon read the update on the front cover of the local newspaper held open on her thighs. The news bringing it all back to the fore, once again.

## INVESTIGATION INTO LOCAL MISSING GIRL TRANSFERRED TO COLD CASE UNIT

Twelve-year-old Seren Lloyd's disappearance in 1994 shocked the community. Her parents are deeply saddened to learn today – the second anniversary of her disappearance – that there has been little response to their nationwide search for information of her whereabouts. Brynmawr area police have decided, for economical purposes, to scale back their investigation.

Detective Superintendent Murrow of Blaenau Gwent Police, in charge of the case said, 'I intend to continue to support her parents, and endeavour to follow every new piece of evidence we come across, but we have decided to downgrade the case due to a shortage of new leads from our most recent petition.'

Bryn appeared in the doorway. 'Not reading that rubbish again, are you?'

'I don't have a say in what they print.'

'I told you, the father did it. It's always the last person you'd expect.'

Stephen Lloyd was an honest, hard-working man. But according to the press, a lousy father. He had a string of children dotted around the country, having got several women pregnant during his job as a lorry driver for a logistics company. He'd lied to the police about where he was when first questioned, not wanting Seren's mother – the only one of his children's he'd ever lived with – to learn about his affair with a tart he'd met up north during one of his deliveries. He was with the woman when his daughter went missing.

Seren's mother, was a self-obsessed looker, who spent far too much time in the hair salon she owned in Cardiff, travelling down each day, forcing her daughter to walk to school and back home alone from the age of ten, against her husband's wishes.

In Rhiannon's view they were both neglectful and selfish, but were they responsible for their daughter's disappearance?

Nobody doubted the kidnapper, if there was one, would be the least likely candidate anyone could consider responsible. Which was probably why he – her abductor was most likely a man – wasn't on the detectives list of suspects. Unless he was someone they'd already interviewed and later dismissed, for reasons the public would never know.

She heard a shuffling then. She'd heard it often. Below her feet, directly underneath the kitchen floor. She was adamant they had rats, but Bryn reassured her he'd found no proof of an infestation.

'What is that noise then?' she said.

Bryn always had an excuse. The water pipes clunking, the floorboards creaking, the joists expanding or retracting. But she daren't go into the basement, where she was positive the sound emanated, and investigate. She hated cramped, dark spaces, and spiders. So, once again, she sent Bryn down to check.

He returned as always looking put out and sounding annoyed. 'I told you, Rhiannon. There's nothing down there.'

But she felt it sometimes, an intuitive tug that pulled her gaze southward. There was something not quite right about the basement.

'You're becoming paranoid.' His face would fill with concern, his brows furrowed, and he'd raise her chin with his workman fingers. 'I'm worried about you, Rhiannon.'

She'd laugh off his accusing stare and kiss him in apology. But it didn't seem to quell the irritated look in his eyes.

And there he was again, down in the basement. Only this time, he wasn't looking for rats, but had decided to go down there to store the boxes of crap he'd started to collect from junk shops and auctions. A telescope with no lens, a hundred glass jars for storing jam she had no time to make, a bin liner full of yellow dusters- those might come in handy, twelve green camping kettles? And two cardboard boxes containing magazines, bottled water, and bedding.

'This has got to stop, Bryn.'

'What has?' he said, climbing up the steps and into

the hall, turning to lock the basement door he told Carys led to a broom cupboard to quell her curiosity and prevent her from attempting to enter his private space. He hated people messing with his things.

'The hoarding,' she said, hoping to halt his compulsion to head back down there with more rubbish.

'Collecting things of use is not the same thing as filling the farm with waste.'

He was stubborn and refused to see things from anyone else's perspective. So as always, she bit her tongue and tried to ignore the urge to nag him that was bubbling up inside her.

She didn't want to fall out with him, today of all days. She hated it when he refused to speak to her. The silent treatment was almost worse than the repercussions Carys experienced when she'd angered her father. Rhiannon would rather have a slanging match with him, but he was very good at getting what he wanted by making you feel at fault without having to voice it.

That, she supposed, was how he got away with things for far longer than anyone else could.

# CARYS

*Brynmawr, Ebbw Vale, Wales, 2018*

PD Ellis, a police dog greeted me at the door of Blaenau Gwent's Criminal Investigation Department headquarters in Cwmbran. He was being taken out for a training day.

The vans rear doors were opened, and he obeyed his command to enter the back where he had a bed, some soft toys, and a bowl of water. He wagged his tail in a happy farewell before the uniformed officer responsible for him closed the doors and checked they were secure before jumping into the front and driving away.

DI Locke led us inside. Lewis walked a few steps ahead of me. The boys were behind me, dragging their feet along the corridor as we were ushered from the entrance and into a room on the ground floor.

We sat on plastic chairs for the doctor, wearing latex gloves, to take swabs from each of us, despite my assertion the boys hadn't touched the baby's remains.

My mouth felt dry afterwards, and I pulled a thread of cotton from the inside of my cheek where it had stuck, dropping it into a wastepaper basket. 'In case of contaminants such as skin cells or hair,' was the only explanation we received. The episode took less than three minutes. Our fingerprints were next.

When we were done, DI Locke led us out of what appeared to have been an interview room and into a more comfortable one with soft chairs, a plant perched on the windowsill, a box of toys on the floor, a spread of children's books on a table, and beanbag in one corner.

The boys, at the detective's advice, growing impatient at the length of our stay due to her request that we speak in private, were sipping cans of diet cola from the vending machine in the waiting area under the watchful eye of the desk clerk behind the hood of her laptop.

DI Locke offered Lewis and me a coffee, which we sipped while she updated us on the progress of the house search. Informing us they'd found something.

'The bones of a child,' she said, her face set, eyes following mine as though trying to read me.

My stomach did a backflip. 'In the paddock?'

'I can't disclose the location.'

'Another baby?' said Lewis.

'No. It looks like a teenager. And it's my understanding that they belong to a female.'

I should have told her about Seren. The suspicion I had of my father's involvement in her disappearance, which I couldn't hide from since CSI had now found a girl's skeleton on his property, and the infants remains that had been swaddled in a green dress like the one she'd been wearing the day she went missing. But my mouth hung open in astonishment and I almost forgot to breathe. 'What uh, happens now?'

'We've dug the garden and sent cadaver dogs into the house, but we haven't uncovered anything else.' There was a silent *yet* in there somewhere.

I couldn't imagine anyone wanting to buy the farm now that its dark history had been brought into the light. There was nothing we could do. We might as well go home. And in that moment there was nothing I wanted to do more.

*You can't*, said the childlike voice inside my head. *Not until you know who the girl was.*

DI Locke glanced from me to Lewis and back again. 'You said when we first spoke to you back at the farm that you'd fallen out with your father. Could you elaborate on that?'

I inhaled, exhaled and bit my lip. 'I fell pregnant with my eldest, Iefan. He went ballistic, so I left.'

'Was he a violent man, Carys?'

'He had a temper, but he didn't express it in public. I wouldn't consider him violent though.'

'He didn't hurt you or your mother?'

'Not my mother. He worshipped her, and I suppose he doted on me too.'

She nodded, temporarily satisfied with my evasive answers and glanced up at the clock on the wall behind me.

'I'm sure you understand I have to ask these questions.'

I nodded, numb.

I left the building ten minutes later, skin clammy, face hot, heart racing. Lewis offered to buy lunch, but I wasn't hungry. I didn't think I could even manage the bottled water he bought us from a petrol station on our way back to the hotel. I recognised the label of the soft water derived from the local spring. I remembered my father buying crates of the same bottles but couldn't recall ever seeing him drink them.

'I want to go back to Bristol,' I said the moment we were inside the car.

'The detectives might want to speak to us again. We should stay here until we find out-'

'If my father was a serial killer?' I'd forgotten the boys were in the back. Thankfully they were both listening to music on their iPods. 'Find out if he murdered a child and a baby and buried them in the paddock?'

He didn't reply.

'What I don't understand is why.'

'I'm positive DI Locke will determine that for us.'

'I've no doubt she will.'

That's what's frightening me.

I stared out of the window, the trees on the side of the road, the buildings, and the sky were a green-brown blur as our car trundled down the hill toward the Beefeater restaurant, situated to the left of the hotel.

Once inside, the boys decided they didn't want to share a table with their preoccupied parents and seated themselves as far away from us as possible to avoid the embarrassment of being bought food when they were of the age that they should be working, able to afford their own.

I'd spent the journey reflecting on the detectives' discovery and shared my thoughts with Lewis. 'The children could be siblings. But how do you suppose they ended up in the paddock?'

'DI Locke said the older kid was a girl, so maybe the baby was hers. She could have been in labour and gone in search of help, had the baby – alive or stillborn – buried the infant, then collapsed in the field and died.'

I struggled to comprehend how no one saw or heard anything if Lewis' hypothesis was proven correct.

'How would a girl have got into the paddock, given birth, dug a grave, and keeled over without my father's or anyone else's knowledge?'

He shrugged and reached out to take my hand in his.

'And why go to the trouble of hiding their bodies if

he hadn't done anything wrong?'

Though their grave digger could just as easily have been my mother.

'*If* they were murdered, whoever was responsible could have buried them before your father was born.'

Though what he said made sense it didn't ease the disconcerting belief that it was my father who had killed them.

Their remains could be ancient, according to the online articles I'd read the night before, unable to sleep. It took just hours for rigor mortis to kick in and merely a couple of weeks to a month for a body to completely decompose, the flesh slipping from the bones like wet crepe paper. Putrefaction left an odour in the air that would alert even the stuffiest of noses to the strong scent of rotting meat. The sound of insects: fly's buzzing overhead, laying eggs in crevices, rats scurrying around the flesh, and the wriggling maggots – once hatched – tunnelling through organs, alerted the nearby wildlife to tear at and feast on whatever remained of the decaying corpse.

It took approximately six months for the dried blackened tendons and cartilage clinging to the bones to completely disintegrate, and a further few for the marrow to harden so that they lightened to a dull grey colour.

At the very least, the girl and the baby had died a year or two ago. But they could just as easily have been buried long before my father inherited the house, from *his* father.

Lewis appeared to have landed on the same theory. 'I suppose it's possible they died around the time your grandfather lived on or even before he obtained, the property.'

'Yeah, I guess.'

All I knew about my paternal grandparents was that they'd lived on the land after the death of my great-grandfather, who'd remained a spinster, for decades. They'd both died before I was born. I saw a grainy photograph of them once. I shared my great-grandfather's reddish hair. I wondered what they would have thought about their land being used to hide children's bodies.

I never knew my maternal grandparents either. The day my mother declared herself one of Jehovah's workers, she turned her back on her parent's sinful lifestyle: they both chain-smoked, regularly drank, and occasionally swore. They died shortly after she joined the fellowship.

Would the police be able to identify the girl and her infant from the bones? Was it possible to determine if the green dress her baby had been covered with and buried in belonged to Seren? Could they discover what had caused their deaths, and who had chosen to hide their bodies?

Though the detective hadn't received confirmation of her identity I'd already ascertained the bones belonged to Seren and the infant was hers.

Which meant she must have been kidnapped by my father and kept somewhere long enough for her to have given birth, because she hadn't been visibly pregnant when she'd disappeared. Perhaps that *was* how she'd died.

But I struggled to comprehend what that meant: that me and my mother had been living with her for at least nine months during which she was alive. That we had no idea what kind of sick monster Bryn Howell was. Or had my mother known? Worse still, did she have something to do with Seren's abduction?

And if they had been killed, why?

Had I narrowly escaped a similar fate?

Of all the twisted, barbaric punishments my father had inflicted upon me as a child that my mother never apologised for allowing, the thought of him harbouring a teenage girl – where? Locking her up in the dark dingy basement? – was far worse.

I thought back to Lewis' intimation regarding voodoo and satanism. Ritualistic abuse came to mind, but I swept the thought away with a long swig of coffee. That was supposedly a myth created in the US when the term sexual abuse first appeared in the public domain as an acceptable conversational topic. Until the exploration of the subject in the eighties, people denied its existence and kept their mouths shut if they witnessed it for fear of being labelled at the very least a tattletale, or worse still- the perpetrator.

I shivered as a blast of cold air fell through the door along with a man wearing a long raincoat.

DI Locke had informed us her colleagues were already sifting through logs of open missing persons cases and filing DNA evidence procured from the fibres present on the skeleton. There were blood splatters visible on the fabric the girl wore that despite its degradation was going to be evaluated.

The pathologist who'd deduced the remains belonged to a girl due to the size of the eye sockets and the shape of her jaw had made it easier for the forensic anthropologist who was in the process of estimating an age and year of death from them, in the hope they'd have something on file to compare the bone samples to.

Doctor Chang's preliminary report of the infant's bones suggested the skull fracture occurred post-mortem. 'Heavy peat,' said DI Locke, by way of explanation.

We left the restaurant to meet a burnt orange and violet sky. Starlings flew past the setting sun in droves, their birdsong carried away with the wind.

I thought the evening sky would make a good picture, but I'd left my camera packed inside the rucksack in our hotel room. Creativity often struck at the most inappropriate time: when I was without the necessary equipment.

I inhaled the cool air deep into my lungs, entered the hotel, and followed Lewis into the lift.

My mobile phone rang the minute we entered our room.

'DS Jones speaking, would you be able to come

back down to the unit in the morning?'

'Yes. Have you found something else?'

'Just routine. We'd like to ask you a few more questions we believe may help us.'

'Okay, sure. Is 10:00am okay?'

'Fine by me. See you then.'

I spent most of the night wondering what they wanted to know, anxious it had something to do with Seren's disappearance. They'd connected the dots. They must have done. I should have told them what I knew or thought I did. By withholding such vital information, I might have held up their investigation.

I knew my concern was ridiculous. It had only been a couple of days. There was no way anything I'd not disclosed could possibly have hindered their case in such a short timeframe. But the guilt was all-consuming.

I gathered the pillow beneath my head and folded it in half. Then I turned to my side, facing the wall, intending to sleep, knowing I wouldn't.

*Who are you protecting, Carys? The grandfather who died before you were born? The grandmother you never met? Your father? Your mother? Or yourself?*

There was another possibility that crossed my

mind. One that caused my heart to race.

Bill Erwin.

My father's taxidermist friend.

He spent a lot of time on the farm as I was growing up. In fact, when I thought about it, he was the only person my parents allowed to step through the front door when he visited because he'd gone to the same school and had grown up with my father. And because he was a Jehovah's witness, like my mother.

A godly man, my mother called him. Cursed, my father said. Because no matter how hard he tried, he could never seduce a woman. That's why he lived alone, or so my father said.

*Thick as thieves those two*, said my mother from the dark recesses of the room.

I clamped my eyes shut against her phantom and tried to ignore the voice, my own imitating hers, from penetrating my eardrums, while whispering 'shut up' into the shadows.

# RHIANNON

*Brynmawr, Ebbw Vale, Wales, 1996*

Carys had fallen out with Zoe. After berating her she'd returned home in a mood and argued with her father. It left a palpable tension in the atmosphere. It didn't help that Rhiannon's head felt like a cement mixer. A dull thudding had accumulated between her temples, making it difficult to see as she straight as she descended the stairs.

Mid-way down, her tingling hand slipped from the bannister. Bryn was always leaving things discarded on the staircase and that day was no exception. Only that time it caused her to stumble down a few steps and fall. By the time she hit the tiled floor, she was already unconscious. Unable to resist he drove her to hospital.

'Type Two Diabetes,' said the doctor she watched

take her pulse through one swollen, black eye.

That must have been what caused her migraines, the muscle weakness, sickness, trembling, numbness, and drowsiness.

'Treatable,' said the doctor, 'with tablets, for now.'

If her symptoms persisted or worsened, he wanted to start her on insulin.

'I'll take the pills, but I won't inject pharmaceuticals into my bloodstream.'

'Your blood glucose level is far too high,' he said, tapping the sheet of paper held in a folder attached to the end of her hospital bed with a piece of string.

'I suppose a hormonal teenager doesn't help,' said Bryn.

'I assure you stress cannot cause this condition Mr Howell.'

Rhiannon saw how uncomfortable the idea that Carys was going through puberty made Bryn.

She let him rant about their daughter's misbehaviour, knowing that to contradict him would give her grief, and smiled wanly when he suggested giving Carys more responsibility around the house.

Bryn looked down at his wife lying in a hospital bed with stiff starched sheets covering her curvy torso and said, 'she can help you with the chores.'

Then he added, 'when you're feeling better, we'll visit Porthcawl. Sun, sea, and sand is what you need. Isn't that right, Doc?'

The doctor said, 'it's a splendid idea.'

So that's exactly what they had done a fortnight later.

The bruising across her eyelid, above her eyebrow and down one side of her forehead had gone down enough to cover the yellowy green tinged skin with foundation. She blended it in with some powder and studied herself in the mirror. Carys left the toilet cubicle of the public lavatory and hovered in the doorway behind her. The swimming costume she was wearing was too small. Rhiannon knew Bryn should have bought her one a size or two bigger.

Outside, bare footed on the hot concrete, Bryn cast a quick glance at his wife, then a longer, more intent look at Carys attempting to cover her chest. The fabric was so tight against her skin it caused the light pink costume she wore to appear almost transparent, and she hadn't even hit the water yet.

Rhiannon glared at Bryn, who appeared to lack understanding as to why she was giving him an I-told-you-so look.

He took Carys' hand as they crossed the cycle lane. Two teenage boys zoomed past them on bikes so fast they almost knocked them over. With one hand unable to cover her developing chest the other gripped tight by her father, one of the boy's wolf whistled at Carys. The other shouted unashamedly that he could see her 'fried eggs.'

'Nobody will see you once you're in the sea,' said Bryn.

But his words didn't quell her mortification, nor the blush that crept up her cheeks.

Rhiannon was embarrassed for her, but she tried hard not to show it. It wouldn't do them any good to bicker out in the street like three commoners.

*Like Zoe's council family*, she heard Bryn say, though his lips weren't moving.

They spent the afternoon sun-bathing, skinny-dipping, eating overpriced ice-creams and soggy, salty, sand-covered chips. When the sky turned grey and clouds gathered ominously above them, leaving their sunspot shaded, they turned to leave before it rained.

Back inside the car, pleasantly tired, Bryn drove

them the forty-mile, hour-long journey home.

That night Carys was in bed before her mother and father, giving Rhiannon ample time to prepare for her trip into town the following morning. The Watchtower leaflets were left, as always, on the step by the back door in a cardboard box, like the ones Bryn reused to store his junk in, that he then dumped in the basement.

She tugged one of the leaflets free from the elastic band holding them together and flipped through it to memorise the message, before sliding it back into the stack. One thousand that time. She'd asked for more, and the senior witness had nodded approvingly.

She carried the box into the kitchen and dumped it onto the countertop. Then there was a resounding thump from somewhere nearby. She stood still and silent for a moment, straining her ears for another sound, sure she'd heard a thud after placing the box down. She picked it up again and slammed it back down. A couple of seconds passed and then there it was again. Two light taps. Like footsteps on concrete. Or was it just an echo?

She was sure the noise had come from the basement.

'Bloody rats,' she hissed, turning to face Bryn, who stood in the doorway.

She walked past him, entered the living room and took her usual seat in front of the television. Bryn followed her like a lost puppy.

'I'll go up and tuck Carys in,' he said, at the start of the news.

'She's too old for bedtime stories.'

He seemed shocked, then annoyed at her comment, but continued up the stairs anyway.

She heard a muffled conversation, mostly Bryn's voice, but through the thick ceiling she couldn't make out what he was saying. There were a few moments of silence, a rustling sound she couldn't be sure hadn't come from the basement, then a bedspring creak, and a lengthy pause before Bryn's footsteps retreated from Carys' bedroom to the bathroom, and several minutes later he returned to the living room.

She knew then. She saw it in his eyes: pupils dilated, slightly bloodshot. And on his face: cheeks flushed, as though he'd been caught out doing something he shouldn't have. There was guilt but not a hint of remorse.

Envy swept across her so that as he wrapped his

arms around her and pressed his body against hers, she fought with all her internal strength not to shove him away and slap his shameless face.

She smelt Carys' bedcovers on his skin. Saw something primal flicker in his eyes as he ripped her shirt, and tugged down her knickers, pushing her against the wall and taking her from behind, fast, and speechlessly.

He slammed into her with none of the care or consideration she was used to during their lovemaking. It was aggressive, emotionless sex. And she wanted it, craved it, savoured the feeling for hours.

Bryn was hers, and she would do anything to destroy anyone who tried to come between them. Even if the woman who wanted to snatch him away from her shared her DNA.

She decided in the moment their bodies parted that if ever Bryn showed any sign of loving Carys more than he loved her, she wouldn't hesitate to tear them both to shreds.

Yes, she was jealous. Green as Ivy. Carys was slimmer than her, younger. Her skin was as smooth as silk, and unblemished. And her eyes were as bright as cut blue glass.

Whereas Rhiannon's skin was sun-damaged and hung loose. Crow's feet spread from the corners of her eyes already, and her waist jutted out and over her hip bones.

But envy is a sin. So she tried to quash the feeling, stuffing it deep down into her core to pretend it didn't exist.

# CARYS

*Brynmawr, Ebbw Vale, Wales, 2018*

The atmosphere in the building was tense and accusing. I didn't bother to accept the coffee from DI Locke that time. Nor did I join in with DS Jones' discussion on the continued bad weather. My coat was soaked through and my feet squelched inside the trainers I'd bought for their memory foam cushioning, hoping the comfort would alleviate some of my constant back pain. I took a seat in the same room I'd frequented the previous day. The fabric around my sodden feet was not Welsh-rain-proof.

'The sun was out until you arrived here,' said DS Jones, reminding me that it had only been four days since we'd left home, and already my life had been turned upside down.

'You wanted to tell me something.'

He sat up straighter. 'We came across some documents in a bin outside.'

'We were de-cluttering,' I spat. I didn't know why I felt as though I should explain our innocent behaviour, but the long gaze he gave made me feel as though I'd done something wrong.

'Did you sift through the items before disposing of them?'

I suddenly felt my neck warming and unbuttoned the top of my jacket. 'Only one box containing some school drawings and a few magazines. None of it seemed relevant so I ordered Lewis to take it outside. We looked at the stables then we found the bones.'

'How many of you lived on the property during your childhood?' said DI Locke.

'Me, my mother, and father.'

'No siblings or cousins?'

'No. Just us. Why?'

'CSI found a collage book filled with newspaper clippings detailing information about a girl called Kavanagh inside a cardboard box that had been stuffed into the bin.'

I silently repeated her name, but it didn't jog a memory.

'The girl would be thirty-three years old now.'

'Would be?'

'She's been missing since 1995 from her home in Abergavenny. She reportedly disappeared just short of a month after her tenth birthday.'

Why would a cluster of articles for a missing girl have been hidden amongst my father's things unless he had an interest in the investigation?

I shifted uncomfortably in my seat. 'There's more, isn't there?'

*What aren't you telling me?*

She turned toward the filing cabinet, selecting a small piece of card or paper from the front of a stack of files, and slid it across the melamine table toward me. It was the photocopy of an aged photograph.

'She looks just like Seren Lloyd,' the words slipped from my mouth uncensored as I stared at the image of Siân.

'We thought so too,' said DI Locke. 'You knew her?'

'No,' I said quickly. 'Seren was in Castle Vale. I went to another school. But the whole town spoke of her often after she . . . went missing.'

'Carys, I know this may be hard to hear but-'

'You think my father took Siân?'

She shared a look with DS Jones then tilted her head westward and smiled sadly. 'We're doing everything we can to find out why those remains were buried on your father's land and to uncover a plausible reason for those newspaper clippings being stored within the property. Our present and probably the most obvious theory is that the individuals living on the farm at the time of the girls' disappearances were responsible for their deaths. Especially considering the discovery of the girls remains, and the collage book containing clips of a girl with identical features to another reported missing from the area the previous year were found on the land.' She paused, added, 'if there's anything you can tell us that you think will help our investigation, I'd appreciate hearing it.'

'It doesn't matter what I think, surely.'

'If something's bothering you, however minuscule you consider it, it might be worth pursuing.'

She studied me. 'Carys?'

I couldn't hold her gaze any longer.

I took a deep breath and told her everything I knew. About my mother's concern over Seren's disappearance and my father's stolen vehicle. The same car I was positive I'd witnessed near to the scene of Seren's abduction.

DS Jones left the room to fetch coffee during a short recess, informing me on his return that Lewis – who had been sitting impatiently in the waiting area – had taken the boys into town for a spot of sightseeing.

By the time I left the police station the rain had stopped, the car park was floodlit, and a mist had descended on the valleys, cloaking everything in fog.

*

Sleep had never come easy to me. I was what some termed a night owl, but once rendered unconscious from exhaustion I struggled to wake. That night was no exception. It wasn't that I was unable to relax, but rather my early morning discovery after hours of trolling through the internet. Finally, around 2:00am I hit on a connection between Seren Lloyd and Siân Kavanagh.

Though they were both taught in different schools in separate towns, at the time they were reported missing they were both taking dance lessons tutored by Gareth Price.

The reputation of the school far surpassed any within a ten-mile radius of the area. Although I was positive the police would already have pursued that line of inquiry, both in the original case, and since receiving the call to attend the farm where it appeared that she was buried. I shivered at the thought.

Gareth had an alibi for the day of Siân's disappearance and a witness confirmed he'd been shopping in Cardiff with his girlfriend at the time she was reportedly abducted.

Gareth was questioned by police for five hours but was quickly eliminated from their enquiries because Seren had failed to arrive to the class he was teaching and, along with the alibi provided by twelve students and their parents and guardians who'd delivered them to and collected them from the dance school, which was when they purported she'd gone missing, there was insufficient evidence to prove he knew where she was or could be responsible for her disappearance.

With no proof of an abduction and no credible leads for her murder the case had remained open. And I assumed the police were hopeful she might still be alive. Though I doubted she could be.

Yet stranger things had happened. Girls and women had escaped captivity years after their abductions. But their stories of incarceration were awful. Most had been starved, beaten, tortured or abused. It was sickening to read such testimonials, but I couldn't stop. I'd been absorbed into the underbelly of a world I'd never experienced, a world I believe we all like to pretend does not exist. I was disgusted by what I'd read, but morbid fascination and a desire to understand the dark side of humanity tempted me in continuing my research.

The witching hour brought my attention to something else right before I plugged my mobile phone into the charger and set my alarm. I noticed that not only did Seren and Siân look almost identical, but they were mirror images of me. They may have disappeared two years apart – Seren was twelve and Siân was ten – but they were the same height, weight, had a light almost translucent skin-tone, and their hair was the same cut and strawberry blonde colour as mine. The only thing that differentiated us was our individually unique features, and eye colour. Seren had an angular nose, a pointed chin, and sky-blue eyes like me. Siân's forehead was covered with ringlets, her face was soft and rounded, and her eyes were large pools of toffee.

I had to squint at the screen of my phone – sleep-deprived and vision blurred – in the near-darkness after switching off the lamp and staring at my mobile for too long but there was no mistaking that the three of us had wavy locks, cut and styled similarly. Far too much so to be a mere coincidence.

I deduced that the person who'd taken them had a *thing* for young girls with rose blonde hair.

I was no longer wondering if my father was the man who'd abducted them, I realised with a moment of clarity in the sleep-deprived abyss I'd enforced upon myself. I was seeking further confirmation that he was the culprit by ignoring the differences between the two cases.

Though it was impossible to forget Gareth Price's potential involvement initially, on some subconscious level I already knew my father was responsible for the girl's abductions and eventual deaths, I was just waiting for the detectives to prove it.

# RHIANNON

*Brynmawr, Ebbw Vale, Wales, 1996*

The term *too close for comfort* could not have been truer when it came to Bryn's relationship with his daughter. He was infatuated with her.

'She's a daddy's girl,' he said. But she was no longer of an age where that term applied.

He followed her around the house like a lovesick puppy. He invaded her privacy whenever he got the chance, and his wife had caught his wandering eye following Carys' movements on several occasions. Rhiannon had no doubt he loved their daughter more than he loved her, but to get Carys to speak up about it would be like attempting to part the sea. Rhiannon felt out of her depth.

If only there was a way of exposing his behaviour without having to force Carys to admit the way her father behaved toward her.

She tried to confront Bryn once, as indirectly as she could get away with. 'Why don't we hire a babysitter and go out for a meal, just you and me?'

'I'm not having some stranger in my house, alone with my daughter.'

*But she's mine too*, Rhiannon wanted to say, but the words froze on her tongue.

'She's my little princess. I don't want her to get hurt.'

'Hurt?'

'Yes. She'll feel abandoned.'

'But we need to spend more time together, just us. It's not healthy for a girl of her age to be around her parents all the time. She needs friends of her own.'

'You and I spend far too much time together. What you need is a hobby. Something to keep your mind off the farm.'

She left the conversation to dry up.

But later she asked Carys if she'd like a lock on her door now that she was grown up, and she expressed a knowledge of her father's unnatural behaviour. 'Yes, please. Zoe's got one. *Her* parents don't barge in on her when they feel like it.'

By parents, she meant father.

Rhiannon noticed Carys' insecurity around men: deliberate acts to hide her body from their lingering gazes one minute and obvious flirting the next. She had convinced herself it was caused by a constant concern due to Bryn's boundaryless behaviour. But when she closer inspected the circumstances and her daughter's outward inappropriateness toward her father it was obvious Carys didn't want to upset him.

Were her seductive impulses a mask used to cover a deep-seated desire not to disappoint him? Was it Carys' fault he couldn't restrain himself?

Despite the awkward lingering glances Rhiannon noted pass between Carys and her father, her daughter was ignorant to the fact it was wrong to jump onto the lap of a stranger during a visit to a family restaurant when on a camping trip, or to sidle between her parents if they dared express their love for each other in front of her with a peck on the cheek or a squeeze of a shoulder. A constant feeling of impending doom weighed on Rhiannon, as if at any moment something would erupt to spoil the delusion that they were a normal loving family.

And it didn't help that Bill Erwin rarely gave them

a moments peace.

After his wife's lengthy illness and eventual death, it was almost as though the man couldn't stand to spend a moment at home and would rather hang around the farm getting under her feet. She couldn't understand it.

She and Bryn were often found in separate areas of the house, he segregated himself from her and Carys even when he had no work to do. It wasn't that they were socially reclusive, he was a businessman after all, and she had God's work to do. But they lived as though unmarried. The bed was all they shared, and what happened between the sheets a chore. However when Bill was there – as he was most days after his wife's funeral – he and Bryn stayed up drinking, discussing motorised agricultural equipment, and generally boring her half to death until the early hours when she'd give up the pretence of hospitality and succumb to another night forced to sleep alone on one side of the cold king-size bed, listening to their muffled chatter and the clink of whiskey glasses through the floor.

As the years had blended into one monotonous list of chores, Rhiannon realised they'd grown too far apart. He preferred the company of her Kingdom Hall companion Bill Erwin, or their daughter Carys to his wife. And that made Rhiannon bitter and resentful.

The day would come, she thought, when the truth would rise between them, burn them, leaving the memory of their marriage, their family, to smoulder like hot ash.

Bryn wielded a power over their daughter like nothing she'd witnessed before. A bond she was unable to explain to her religious leader, and so, like her daughter, Rhiannon suffered in silence until she could stand their unhealthy living arrangements no more. Nor was she strong enough to break it.

'I'm leaving you, Bryn,' she said, stood in the living room doorway wearing her coat, a suitcase at her feet.

It was a test. At least that was what she was aiming for.

'What about Carys?'

'It's always about *her*, isn't it? What about me, Bryn?'

'What about you?'

She tugged on the handle of her suitcase, intending to carry it out of the door with her but it snapped and dropped from her hand to the carpet.

'That's a sign,' he said, pointing at the bag that refused to go with her.

'I have nothing to stay for.'

'How am I supposed to keep things running, take care of Carys without you?'

'You'll cope.'

'You're not thinking clearly. You can't just leave us here.'

She sighed. 'Why ever not? You give *her* more attention than you give to me.'

'That's because she's a child.'

'Your priorities are warped. You should put us first.'

'Quoting from that book of yours again,' he scorned.

'Yes. Because it's The Truth.'

He moved toward her, pulled her close, and lowered his voice. 'Stay. I don't know what I'd do without you.'

And so reluctantly, she did. Through fear that his words were a warning, a threat. Because what would he do to Carys if she was no longer around to prevent it?

# CARYS

*Brynmawr, Ebbw Vale, Wales, 2018*

I'd become obsessed with the case since learning the details given to me by DI Locke just hours before they were printed online. The child's bones that they'd found in the paddock belonged to a Caucasian girl who was approximately twelve years old when they believed she'd died. She was four feet ten inches tall and weighed roughly five stone. She'd had an abscess below one of her top, front milk teeth that the forensic anthropologist determined must have been removed to accommodate the adult tooth that had grown partway through the gum at the time of her death, which they estimated to have been between the years 1950 and 2000 due to the approximate state of skeletal deterioration.

I knew dental records could be used to identify the

girl, and from what I'd read they were highly accurate. It was only a matter of days before the detectives would learn the child's name- if she'd been registered with a UK dentist. Had she been of European decent it was still possible, though might take slightly longer to uncover. And it would prove harder to disclose if she was a private rather than an NHS patient due to the Data Protection Act.

I wasn't sure how I felt about that. Glad in a way because that meant her parents would know for certain what had happened to their daughter, would be able to give her a ceremonial goodbye, and they'd have the closure they needed to move forward with their lives- if they were still alive. But scared too. Because once named I'd know for sure if the girl had died before or after my birth. If her death had been naturally caused or deliberate. If she *had* been killed whether her murderer was one of my own family members. And if the person who'd taken her life had also been responsible for burying her.

With a sixty-year window, I was still no closer to knowing which one of my great-grandparents, grandparents, or parents were living on the farm at the time of the girl and/or the infant's death.

I was glad to be away from it all.

Iefan followed me down to the old ironworks where I'd chosen to drive to escape the lunacy of our situation.

The ground was flat and tinged coal grey or black depending on where you stood and how the sunlight caught the mineral fragments on the earth, which when the sun caught them mimicked spilt petrol and gave the appearance of a rainbow.

The area was desolate; void of human traffic or the sound of tyres on tarmac. The air seemed to vibrate; I could almost feel the residual energy emanating off the land that had been trodden on by miners carrying iron ore in wheelbarrows, digging the underground rocks with a pitchfork.

Blaenavon grew from a small market town to one of the many metal mining hotspots during the industrialisation of Wales. The ironworks, like the steel and copper quarried in the east, attracted men- mostly from as far north as Liverpool, or Plymouth in the south.

In the distance I could see the balance tower. A colossal stone-built hub for separating and weighing up the precious – heavy, in weight and worth – metal.

To my right, acres of tall grass, sun-starved and yellowed, rustled in the wind. Midway down the valley the air roared in my ears and stroked my face as though unsure what to commit to.

I caught a look of serenity on Iefan's face. His pale cheeks were pinched, and his T-shirt hugged his muscled forearms.

During the early years of motherhood, we spent a lot of time on our own together. I pushed Iefan on swings, strolled through the centre of Broadmead with him wrapped up from the biting snow in a buggy, taught him to swim in the lido on day trips to Swindon, chased him through Leigh woods, held his hand as we ambled along the River Avon, sailed boats we'd made from Sellotaped ice lolly sticks and paper along the Portishead lake, covered him in sun cream only for him to wash it off in the sea on hot summer days in Weston-Super-Mare, and raced him home after a picnic in Vassals Park. He was always so calm, so focussed, and even when he was, he never looked troubled. His eyes flit from the houses below to the cavernous hills guarding us from above, and I wondered what he thought, how he felt about our current situation.

Iefan's was an empathic soul, he understood implicitly when to speak and when to stay quiet. So when he crossed his legs and sat with his back straight facing the scrappy mountainside, patted the damp weed-riddled grass beside him, and invited me to join him I knew he had something important to say. I swallowed hard, afraid he'd begin asking about his grandfather- who he'd never known, and was pleasantly surprised when instead he said, 'places absorb emotions.'

'People can too.'

'We project them as well.' He paused, sweeping the horizon with the same faraway look I gave when embroiled in thought. When searching my surroundings for the perfect shot, annoyed I hadn't thought to bring my camera up there with me- again.

I was just starting to feel my blood pressure lower. The scent of morning dew on the wild grass, the air clean and fresh with the promise of spring. Then he spoke again, breaking the spell. 'I got the feeling you weren't happy here. Even before all this ...'

I looked across at him. He was staring down at a clump of brittle grass, the crushed dandelions beneath our legs. 'It's not the farm, it's-'

'Him.'

I nodded, my fingers winding around a stem. I absentmindedly dug my nails into the earth. They came up soot black.

'People are complicated. No one is all good or all bad.'

'I guess not.' I picked at the head of a daisy. Pulling a couple of petals off the flower at a time. *He loves me, he loves me not, he loves me, he loves me not, he . . .*

Iefan's voice faded into the background. My hands shrunk, as I squashed the yellow seeds of pollen between my fingertips.

I saw my mother picking daffodils from the corner of the road wishing she'd pay as much attention to me as she did to the fucking flowers. She gathered a bunch in her hand and waved me off when I suggested adding the poppies I'd collected from the garden. 'You're not supposed to pick those,' she said, face screwed up tight to avert her eyes from the sun.

'I think they look pretty.'

'Yes, but I only want yellow in the vase.'

What the elder of her church wanted he got. While I was left at home with *him,* my mother flirted with her faith.

Later that evening when she returned home from her meeting, reiterating the crap she'd been discussing with her friends to my uninterested father she found the vase she'd been keeping them in smashed, a puddle of water on the carpet, the daffodil heads folded over the edge of the table, wilting like my childhood.

\*

'What do you think?' Iefan's voice cut through the memory like broken porcelain, and the splintered heat of my mother's blame-filled glare disintegrated from my mind.

'Sorry, I didn't catch what you were saying.'

'The haunted shaft.'

'Oh yes, the miners who died beneath the rubble.'

'Was it here?'

'No. I've never been here before.'

'You haven't?'

'That's why I brought you up here. I've always wanted to see the place.'

'Now you have, what do you intend to do?'

He was expecting me to reply with something like,

*sit and listen to the trees rustling in the breeze, feel the body of mother earth beneath my hands.* Instead I rose from the spiky grass that had left lines to imprint the backs of my thighs and motioned toward the car. 'Let's get something to eat. I'm starving.'

We sat opposite one another swapping banal conversation over a glass table in a pub garden. The scent of wood-smoked beef being barbequed on a griddle in one corner made my mouth water, while a trellised wall lined with blush pink roses that hadn't yet bloomed reminded me of the perfume my mother had worn and caused my chest to tighten. Iefan smoked a cigarette, took a swig of the lemonade I'd bought him, and tapped the table leg with his foot.

I looked up at him, smiled.

'You're miles away.'

I was distracted. My attention span was at an all-time low. It wasn't much better when we returned to the hotel. I couldn't evade the memories that our circumstances had awoken.

The sky had turned grey, my hands were greasy from burger fat, and a thread of cheese clung to the sleeve of my coat. I wanted to erase the prickling sensation of discomfort that clung to my skin. But even after a shower I couldn't shake the feeling of being contaminated by the image of my former self aggressively yanking the heads from daisies while asking the universe whether my father loved me or not.

Didn't little girls question the adoration of their crush in the same way?

# RHIANNON

Rhiannon's eyes skittered across the room. She took a quick glance at everyone seated around her, as still as statues, focussed intently on the circuit elder of the Watchtower Society who revealed a persuasive commentary of the video they'd just finished viewing.

She closed her eyes and allowed the words to soak through her skin and seep into the marrow of her bones.

*A mild answer turns away rage, but a harsh word stirs up anger. Put away from yourselves every kind of malicious bitterness, anger, wrath, screaming, and abusive speech, as well as everything injurious.*

Bryn was a grown man who knew how to behave. She must not question him, nor implore him to act how she wished him to. She must surrender her will to Jehovah. He would know what to do with Bryn and how to sanctify him of his wickedness. It was not her job to steer him away from evil and toward redemption.

At the end of the service, she helped stack the chairs and drag the tables back to the far wall. She dried the cups while one of the older women washed them. Then she hung around outside, feeling the cold breeze on her neck as she waited for Bill to exit the hall.

'How are you keeping, Rhiannon?'

'Good.'

He gave her a quizzical look that made her feel exposed. 'I'll walk you to your car.'

She remained several steps behind him. Didn't want anyone whispering rumours about them behind her back.

He stopped in front of the bonnet of his red MG. 'What's happening, darl?'

'I feel this distance from Bryn. It's as though there's a wall between us that I can't penetrate.'

'Uh-huh.'

'Bryn adores Carys. Our bond has never been very strong, but I feel I'm losing them both.'

'Private matters should be spoken about between you.'

'I'm sorry. I know I shouldn't discuss our intimacies with you, but he doesn't notice me anymore. I feel invisible. How can I begin a conversation when Bryn tries skirting the issue whenever I bring it up?'

'It is for God to decide,' he said, kicking up dirt as he toed the gravel, like he did when preparing himself to recite a bible verse. She closed her eyes and listened. 'Jealously without foundation is wrong and lacking love, and it can result in ruin to the marriage.'

She made a silent vow that if she felt Bryn's love slipping again, she'd provide service to those in greater need. Something she'd been encouraged to do, to eradicate her self-will when she'd had doubts about ending her career. It should help her to deal with this complexity too, she thought.

She entered the farm just as the dying sun winked at her one last time before disappearing through a wall of coral clouds. She eased off her walking boots and followed the sound of the television, finding Bryn asleep on the sofa in the living room. She inched close to him and switched it off. He murmured incoherent words and snorted.

She couldn't allow him to lay there all night, his neck crooked, arm hung twisted, the back of his hand grazing the thin carpet with each inhalation. She ran her fingers through his thick sideburns, and down his bushy beard, noting the receding hairline and the few strands of grey up top. They were both aging fast and she hated to think of them growing old together, Carys leaving home, just her and Bryn drying up alone like two pieces of rotting apple forgotten at the bottom of a fruit bowl.

Their marriage was one of convenience. Her family were poor, her father sick and her mother going blind. It was the financial security she wed him for. Bryn was a hard worker, a businessman, a dedicated employer, and a determined man. Much like his father she'd ascertained. Bryn was confident he could give her what she needed, but he wanted a child to inherit the land his grandfather had bestowed upon *his* father. His ideals were old fashioned that way.

Bryn's brothers wouldn't see a penny of the money left in his father's wake, and so knowing they would be financially well off he encouraged Rhiannon to be a mother. He'd been expecting a boy and she was pleasantly surprised to find his eyes light up at the prospect of bringing up a girl.

She was glad at first, but when she saw how Bryn looked at her compared to the way he fixated on Carys it was hard not to become bitter, which caused her to alter her style and mannerisms to better please her husband. It rarely worked, but she continued anyway. A new skirt here, a different colour eyeshadow there, an expensive perfume, or a more fashionable pair of shoes.

'Where are you going to go dressed like that?'

'I thought you'd like it,' she said, eyes roaming down her full-length, lemon-coloured, tunic dress.

'It'll get clotted with mud while you're mucking out.'

He was right.

*Adorn yourself with respectable dress. Appropriate, and modest.*

Being a farmer's wife wasn't part of the deal she'd made as he slipped the sapphire ring onto her finger. She'd been promised stability, a continually substantial income, but what she'd got was dirty fingernails and cheaply made hats bought in a charity shop that blew off her head at the threat of a gale because they were second-hand and never quite fit.

While Bryn sat alone in his upstairs office, she was responsible for tending to the sheep, hens, pigs, and foals, as well as the housework, and the childcare. Just like his late mother had.

She'd chosen marriage and family over a well-paid job because that was what God wanted. She should be grateful for her achievements, not jealous of others. But the weight of it all fell heavy on her shoulders, and it sometimes felt as though it was dragging her down.

She looked at her sleeping husband, roused him, and led him up the staircase. His breathing heavy, footsteps disjointed from having been woken up and escorted into their bedroom where he fell on top of the duvet, without uttering goodnight.

How she wished he'd gaze into her face adoringly as he'd once done without her express request. How she longed for the subtle dance between a hug and making love. Or the bitter taste of shaving balm on her lips as he pressed his mouth against hers. The devotion in his touch as their bodies yielded to one another beneath the covers. But it was gone, all of it.

She wondered what a man did with himself when

he was no longer attracted to his wife. Had Bryn found himself another way to relieve his desires, and did it involve another woman?

The fear kept her awake most of the night. She tried to sleep, but the images danced across her eyelids for hours. She must have drifted off because she awoke to the darkness in a cold lonely bed. She heard Bryn's low voice muttering something she was too afraid to hear through the gap in the door.

When it grew silent but she hadn't heard the clack of the receiver being replaced, she presumed rather than speaking to someone on the phone Bryn must have been comforting Carys, tucking her back into bed. She'd been infected with the nightmares for years but could never remember when they'd begun. Rhiannon could though. It was just after she'd turned six.

# CARYS

*Brynmawr, Ebbw Vale, Wales, 2018*

The morning was warm and dry, and I had a good feeling that day would not be filled with another flood of negativity. I rose, dressed, enjoyed a Continental breakfast, and took pleasure in the taste of strong bitter coffee on my tongue.

Lewis knocked on the boys' door to invite them out for a trip to the beach.

The sky was blue and devoid of clouds. The coastline split evenly in two; the sea a sheer glimmering silk against the velvet soft horizon.

Lewis' suggestion to visit Porthcawl on the Vale of Glamorgan served only to solidify the knowledge that it was possible for there to be two versions of the same thing. I looked right to the choppy Welsh waves smacking against the rocks below the craggy cliffs.

Then left to the sound of the saltwater gently lapping against the shore, soothing my soul, like a blanket of calm washing over me.

The sound of my mobile phone disturbed the peace, and it took me a few moments to recognise the shrill, my mind elsewhere, bare feet moving lazily through the coarse sand. The withheld number sent a fizzle of irritation through my muscles, causing them to tense as I answered.

I heard a restrained sigh down the line. 'We've received a report from the lab concerning the DNA samples. Are you free to talk?'

I mumbled a reply, not thinking for one minute that what DI Locke was about to impart would put an entirely different spin on the investigation.

'The green dress used to cover the infant has been positively identified as belonging to Seren Lloyd.'

The dark stain on it must have been her blood.

My breath caught in my throat.

'However, our forensic odonatologist has examined the child's teeth, and has determined the teenager's bones belong to a missing girl called Ella James, reported to have disappeared around 1995 from care. Social services believed the eleven-year-old had run away from home. A witness claimed they'd seen her in Porthcawl around the time police were searching for her.'

'Porthcawl?'

'Yes, does the area have any significance to your father?'

'I don't think so. I mean we visited the place a couple of times. In fact . . .' *Should I tell them I was there now?* I did.

'We've never been able to identify the female caller to confirm the relevance of the sighting. Though it seems now that she misidentified the girl.'

*Did your mother report seeing Ella alive after her disappearance to throw the police off the scent of her decaying corpse?*

'We've also been able to prove the baby, a girl, was Ella's through mitochondrial – that's maternal – DNA indexing.'

Something told me DI Locke was saving the worst until last. 'The baby shares your own genetic code, Carys.'

Ella's baby was my sister.

The phone slipped from my hand and Lewis caught it before it became submerged in wet sand. I stumbled away from the boys, their worried expressions burning into me as I found a suitable place to drop. Lewis thanked DI Locke for passing the information on and ended the call before hurrying toward me, gripping my shoulders in his strong hands while I remained bent over, shaking and retching with tears streaming down my face.

'Carys?' Lewis wrapped his arms around me as I heaved and sobbed onto his chest, leaving his T-shirt stained with snot and tears, staring blankly at the boys who looked as though they didn't know what to do- walking toward me only to step back again. Eventually, Iefan brought his arms around my waist, and held me at arms-length from behind. Rhys put a hand on my forearm and squeezed through the fabric of my jacket.

I waited until the boys had turned, reassuring them I was okay, though I wasn't. Watched them edge back to the sandy shore in search of jellyfish, out of earshot, before I spoke. 'Bryn's the baby's father.'

He looked confused.

'The girls name was Ella James. She went missing from state care in 1995 at the age of eleven. Her daughter, the infant, was my sister.'

He shook his head, eyes wide with disbelief. 'Fucking hell, Carys. That means . . .'

He couldn't finish the sentence, and I didn't want to do it for him.

My father had abducted an eleven-year-old girl, holding her captive for long enough to get her pregnant before killing her and their baby and burying them in the paddock of the house he shared with me and my mother.

'The dress belonged to Seren Lloyd. She disappeared the summer of my twelfth birthday. She was my age . . .'

After several minutes of silence, Lewis taking far longer to digest the information than I had, I prised myself out of his tight grip and stood swaying on the rough, gritty sand.

The day was ruined. So much for a pleasant trip out of town.

Lewis took the steering wheel and drove us back to the hotel in silence. I gazed through the windscreen at the flash of crystalline aqua as it was replaced by woodland, farmland, the river, then the beacons; dark craggy rocks and heather interspersed with roadworks and service stations. Soon, the muddied River Usk was visible through a wall of treelined houses that splintered off from the A-road. Finally, we arrived back at the hotel. The moment we entered the building, Rhys announced he was hungry, and I realised we hadn't eaten, didn't get to enjoy a crispy battered cod and a mound of hot salty chips on the seafront as I'd promised.

There was a visceral sense of foreboding in the air as we mounted the staircase, changed into something less comfortable, presenting to the world that we were not outsiders haunted by a dark, disturbing truth.

The unwelcoming stares I received as we headed down to the restaurant for a bite to eat confirmed that the staff at least already knew who we were, why we were lodging there, and what my father had done.

I tried not to allow the darting looks and constant whispers to prevent me from pretending to enjoy my meal of over-cooked steak and ale pie and re-heated potatoes, but I struggled to swallow the food. It clogged in my throat, blocking the words I wanted to but couldn't- voice.

I looked across the table. Iefan stared down at his plate, dragging a chip through his gravy. Rhys stared at me, looking away the moment our eyes met. I stabbed my fork into the pastry, felt it thick on my tongue the moment I slid it into my mouth. I chewed without tasting. Unsaid words building between us.

The moment I waved goodbye to the boys to retreat to our hotel room, I could contain my feelings, the punishing atmosphere of the hotel, and the knowledge I'd accumulated, no more. 'Anyone would think *I* was the murderer.'

'They'll soon grow bored, find something else to occupy their gossiping mouths.'

'Not while the investigation is ongoing, while we're here.'

'None of this is your fault. Why are you punishing yourself?'

I made for the door because to answer Lewis would have led to an admission I wasn't prepared to give.

'Where are you going?'

'I can't sit here all afternoon like a spare bit. I need to think.'

*I must walk off this awful feeling of guilt that keeps reaching out at me and threatening to pull me under.*

I stepped out into the corridor and bumped into a

chambermaid. Did they still call them that? She looked startled. 'You shouldn't jump out at a woman with a spray bottle of bleach in her hand,' she laughed. But before I could reply, her smile faded, and her eyes narrowed. 'You're that Bryn's daughter, aren't you?'

'I . . .'

'What kind of sick fuck buries kids in their garden?' She turned, tutted, and I got the feeling she would have spat at me if she could have got away with it.

I was frozen to the spot as I watched her drag the vacuum down the hall, a carry case filled with gloves, bathroom cleaner, and cloths bouncing against her thigh as she hurried down the corridor to unlock the door to a room three down from ours, snapping the lock in place behind her.

Lewis stood in the doorway, mouth agape.

It was only a matter of time before the news spread like wildfire across Ebbw Vale. That night would spark national media interest, and by morning my father's face would be plastered across the front pages of newspapers throughout the country. If everyone in the hotel recognised me that meant someone had already posted a photograph of me – daughter of the serial killer – somewhere, and it wouldn't take long before the press arrived at the hotel.

For my name to be associated with my fathers was an insult, but for my husband and sons to have their lives torn to shreds by the media compromised our privacy. Didn't we have rights?

All this observation was too much, too soon. I couldn't deal with it.

I took off with Lewis at my heel, down the corridor, jumping the stairs two at a time, like I expected my mother Rhiannon had the day she fell and finally learned what was wrong with her. I almost tripped through the open door of the entranceway, out onto the street to breathe in the cool air. Gulping it into my lungs like sweet tasting tobacco.

This is it, I thought. My father's secret is out. It's over. I can't hide from it anymore.

# RHIANNON

*Brynmawr, Ebbw Vale, Wales, 1998*

Carys was a difficult child to tame. Energetic, free-spirited, impulsive, and by the time she'd turned sixteen she was heading down a dangerous path. Bunking off school. Smoking and drinking with her friends. She was far too advanced for her age.

Despite acting sweet and virgin-like around her father, word spread that Carys' promiscuity was the reason Zoe was no longer allowed to invite her out. But Carys didn't seem to care anymore. Not about the loss of her best friend or her sullied reputation as the girl that no boy would want to bring home to meet his parents. Carys was the one that the mothers of the lads back at school warned them about. Rhiannon heard the rumours spread around the neighbourhood. Carys was already tarred as a slag.

Rhiannon found the CD's, chocolate, and Mizz magazines under Carys' bed. There was no boyfriend that Rhiannon knew of, but Carys often spent too much time hanging around the local shopping precinct and in the park on the estate several miles away with a group of teenage girls and lads a few years older than her, so there was every chance there was one she didn't want her parents to be aware of. One of them must have been supplying her with gifts.

The one time that Carys had returned home stinking of cannabis Rhiannon advised her to get changed before her father arrived, but she just giggled and said that nothing Bryn did to her now would matter anymore, that she'd been numbed down from years of his sexualized discipline and revealed to Rhiannon something that suggested she almost liked it.

'At least he pays attention to me.'

But seeking affection from her father by making him angry enough to force her over his knee was not the kind of attention a normal sixteen-year-old girl should aim for, and so, as she lost her focus in the lead up to her GCSE's, Rhiannon suggested Carys find a job to get her out of the house in the evening. She didn't need to say the real goal was to ensure Carys was as far away from her father as possible; when Rhiannon was busy in the fields and couldn't keep an eye on them indoors. But rather than bite back with a cutting remark as usual, Carys agreed.

Seeing pound signs floating in front of her eyes, Carys began working part-time (after school and Saturdays) in a book shop in town. It was there, she told Rhiannon a few months later that she'd met Lewis. The laid-back builder's labourer who earthed her.

But Rhiannon didn't discover her daughter's pregnancy nor know it was the cause of her rush to escape Ebbw Vale until much later. Had she discovered what she suspected earlier it would have destroyed their upcoming nuptials.

'I'm going to marry him, mother.'

'You're so young. What do you know about love?'

'It's not always about love. Sometimes we have to sacrifice what we want to get what we need.'

Rhiannon thought about her own motive for getting hitched so soon after meeting her husband and in that moment, everything slotted into place.

'Is the baby his?'

'It has to be, I haven't slept with anyone else.'

Rhiannon could hear the discomfort in her daughter's voice, could see her unconvincing eyes sparkle as they did whenever she lied, but to admit Carys was pregnant with another man's child would force them both to accept there could only be one possible alternative biological father, and the thought was too painful for Rhiannon to acknowledge. So she locked her feelings of fear and anger up tight. She'd far rather they festered inside of her than word the awful truth.

At least out of the house and away from Wales, Carys and her baby would have a chance at a normal life. Rhiannon didn't think for one moment that secrets like hers could continue to wrap their tentacles around you, dragging you down, and continuing to destroy you long after you'd left the situation in which you were intent on running from. Carys didn't appear to understand that either.

Rhiannon assured herself Carys' decision to leave home was the right thing to do, that it would benefit them all. Rhiannon would have no need to worry herself sick over her daughter getting knocked up by some loser. The worst had already happened. Surely that was a positive thing?

She'd expected Bryn to rant and rage at Carys' choice to leave home at just sixteen years of age and move to the city with a boy only a year older than her with just a rusty old mark three Escort his father had given him for the drive to Bristol and his last lot of wages from the builder's yard to his name. But Bryn's deliberate lack of obvious annoyance was more disconcerting. His silent disdain meant he was plotting revenge. She was glad Carys had no intention of giving her father a forwarding address.

Bryn entered the room, face set in cold impassivity. She followed his eyes down to Carys' expanding waistline wondering if Bryn knew what was inside her stomach and if he'd put it there.

Though it pained her to admit, the affection and attention he plied Carys with, she could see now, was not an act of love. He'd been abusing her.

Rhiannon had wondered many times if her paranoia would drive a further wedge between her and her husband, but it seemed he was more than capable of doing that himself.

She waved goodbye to her daughter from the sofa she felt incapable of leaving due to the suffocating exhaustion of sickness hanging over her. She feared the smile Carys gave her might be the last she ever saw.

'You'll visit, won't you?'

She didn't reply.

Rhiannon fell asleep around midday. She heard Carys return from the book shop later, but she hadn't the energy to open her eyes least of all to raise her head and speak. She fell back to sleep listening to the ticking of the grandfather clock in the hall striking away the dying hours.

# CARYS

*Brynmawr, Ebbw Vale, Wales, 2018*

Of all the places to hear my father's name alongside Ella James' the radio was the last I'd considered. I heard enough before Lewis switched the channel over as we left the hotel to book ourselves into a B&B in Maindee, Newport. An area unfamiliar to me, and less likely to arouse an influx of press at the doors like the ones we'd just barged past to escape the Premier Inn in Brynmawr. Cameras flashing and unanswerable questions being slung at me from every conceivable direction as I darted beneath Lewis' coat to hide my face. The face that would stare back at me the following day from The Argus online.

Lewis drove around for a while and parked up at the top of a park where Beechwood trees shaded the sun from our faces as we strolled toward a bench nestled beneath a grove beside a stream.

'Can't we go home?' said Rhys.

Iefan so far had remained silent, but I could see the cogs turning in his head as he tried to come up with a reason to argue against his brother's question.

'We can't love, not yet.'

I knew he missed his girlfriend. But we still had the police to deal with. And Lewis would have had to book another fortnight off work if our stay had been extended any longer due to the building case against my father and the re-investigation into Seren's disappearance.

I notified DI Locke about our change of address. A large Victorian three-storey building opposite a mobile phone shop, with an unsavoury view of the viaduct to the left of our bedroom window. Although there was no possibility the trains would keep me awake at night if sleeping continued to evade me.

I'd taken to reading until my eyes fell heavy and I slumped into a sudden deep three-hour-long sleep with an open novel rested over my face, preventing Lewis from witnessing my eyes spring wide several times throughout the night as the nightmares I hadn't experienced for months returned with a vengeance.

While I spoke to the detective earlier that day, I could hear DS Jones in the background asking for directions to a property near to my father's house. I hadn't connected the dots until Gwenda called my mobile sometime later to inform me the police suspected Bryn Howell had kidnapped, impregnated and murdered Ella James, and either her small body hadn't been able to cope with the stress of childbirth, so she'd died during or shortly afterwards or he'd decided to get rid of the evidence of his crime by adding the murder of Ella and his new-born daughter to his list of offences.

What I wanted to know was how well Gwenda knew my father, but she was vague in her reply, skirting the issue with snippets of information she'd garnered from the journalists as she passed the farm while walking her dog twice daily.

Seren Lloyd's body hadn't been found on the property, but the newspaper articles that mentioned Siân Kavanagh's disappearance suggested *she'd* at one time been present at the farm. Someone in CID must have divulged their discovery of the collage book containing newspaper articles to them. Which meant the police were building a strong case against my deceased father for Ella's abduction, false imprisonment, rape, and murder, and the death of their unnamed daughter, in the hope of dredging up enough circumstantial evidence to convict him for Seren and Siân's deaths. Despite the fact he was now dead and would of course go unpunished. DI Locke had already insinuated to the possibility Bryn had abused others, and you didn't need a degree in crime and policing to know they suspected my father had abducted and sexually assaulted Seren and Siân before murdering them too. But I wasn't ready to face her questioning tone when she expressed a wish to delve deeper into my relationship with him. It was humiliating enough knowing my mother must have been aware of Bryn's actions and had done nothing to prevent them, and I'd already accepted she could have been involved in befriending the girls, luring them to the house and . . .

I couldn't imagine the rest. It was too painful.

But the way DI Locke spoke to me, I felt almost betrayed by her softly spoken words of useless comfort.

I wasn't the one on the stand so why did I always feel as though I should defend myself?

I returned to the B&B after a jaunt through the town, taking off to investigate the area. I marched on past the shops, turned right, continued uphill, rounded the corner at a small roundabout and through a housing estate that took me down to Carleon Road. I followed the A-road past a car dealership as it wound toward the river where St Julian's merged with Carleon, the muddy water beckoning me. The air unpolluted, birdsong in the trees, a light breeze skimming my hair from my eyes and caressing my face.

I found myself staring into the water beside a quaint pub where a paddle boat bobbed up and down on the surface. I remained there, on the verge of the mud banks until I felt my limbs relax, the muscles around my spine re-adjusting themselves, my posture attempting unsuccessfully to realign itself.

The B&B was far cooler upon my return. Clouds had gathered above me as I stretched my limbs, feet aching from the six-mile hike.

Inside the large homely room that smelt of lavender I fell onto a chair facing the road and remained there, staring through the window at the traffic until Lewis appeared beside me, holding out my phone.

'Carys, it's Emma.'

Me and DI Locke were on informal speaking terms.

It seemed no matter where I went, I couldn't escape the tiresome deeds of my father long enough to forget about them.

'Can you drive down to Cwmbran in the morning?'

'I'll speak to you here, at the B&B.'

'How about somewhere out of the public eye? A quiet backstreet café perhaps?'

'Costa. 10:00am.'

I hung up before my voice cracked.

Even before the police had suggested it, I already had an understanding that there was a sexual motive in a high percentage of cases where children were abducted and killed. The facts were evident my father was a sexual predator who took pleasure in abusing the trust and snatching away the innocence of young girls. And I had no doubt he'd taken satisfaction in causing them pain. He gained pleasure in making *me* cry.

His discipline was ruthless, and embarrassing, and

he seemed to enjoy it. I winced from the memory.

Lewis brought me a cup of tea, asked if I wanted to talk.

'No.'

What good would peeking around the corner into the past do me?

I was older, stronger, and my father was no longer alive to frighten me. I was not that terrified, confused girl anymore. So why did I still feel as though I was gagged into silence?

# BRYN

*Brynmawr, Ebbw Vale, Wales, 1998*

Rhiannon refused medical assistance for as long as she could get away with. Bryn hoped she would see the error in her thinking before it was too late, but that September, Rhiannon fell into a coma, one she remained in until she died.

'You should have made her take insulin,' Carys screamed.

'You know she wouldn't have listened to me. She was brainwashed by that religious sect.'

'Damn you both to hell.'

'That's no way to speak to your father. Have you forgotten that while you're under my roof you live by my rules?'

She glared at him, scowling, fists pumping. 'I won't be here for much longer.'

'You're not leaving, Carys.'

'How are you going to stop me, chain me up in the attic?'

He tried not to show his shock over her choice of words, but it was difficult to see anything behind her furious eyes.

Did she know about the girl?

That's impossible, he thought. He was so careful.

'Why are you in such a hurry to leave?'

She didn't reply, but as she turned toward the door to abscond, the hem of her coat – the one she'd worn like a second-skin indoors all winter – caught on the door handle, forcing it aside as she tugged to free the fabric, and he saw her stomach had bloomed.

Carys was always a healthy weight so it was not impossible she'd been over-indulging the chocolate he bought to keep her quiet, but heat rose to his cheeks as he considered the possibility that she was pregnant.

Was that the cause of all those lingering looks and whispered conversations she shared with her mother?

I'll kill him, he thought. I'll murder the bastard who's violated my daughter.

Then another thought came to him, hot and frightening, choking his response as she made for the door, exclaiming she was going to stay over a friend's house for the night, that he was not to try to prevent her or follow her there.

'You are too young.'

She stalled in the doorway and with eyes watering in anger said, 'I might be too young for a lot of things *father*, but that doesn't mean I can't do them, does it?'

'Now your mother's not here it's my duty to protect you.'

Carys' shoulders shook as she tried and failed to restrain her rage, wanting to appear mature and confident. But he could see past that to the little girl he'd read bedtime stories to. The little girl who tugged on the sleeve of his jacket and who followed him around the house like a lamb. The little girl who used to like sitting on his lap to watch the sports programmes just to feel the warmth of his chest as she nestled under his arm. The little girl he thought would always be there to love him unconditionally.

But that little girl was gone. And in her place stood a sullen teenager he no longer had any use for, threatening to leave him.

'The only person I need protecting from is you,' she cried, as she turned her back on him and stormed out the door.

He kicked a Yellow Pages across the room, swiped ornaments from the cabinet onto the floor as he crossed the carpet to knock everything that stood on the shelving unit onto the floor. He picked up a family photograph and hurled it across the room.

He didn't harm her. He couldn't, wouldn't do that to his precious Carys. Never. What was she saying?

He twisted her words round in his head. He was coming loose at the seams, falling apart.

As far he was concerned, if that was how she wanted to play it, then she was dead to him. And that was okay because without her or Rhiannon around he was free to choose someone to take their place.

That night he lay in bed staring at the empty space beside him and stroked the sheet as he contemplated what his next move would be.

# CARYS

*Brynmawr, Ebbw Vale, Wales, 2018*

I awoke sensing a presence in the room. Once again trapped in a nightmare with no escape.

Like always it began with a coldness creeping along my body, from my neck to my feet, as though someone had yanked the covers from the bed. I was paralysed with fear and my chest felt tight. A heavy weight had fallen over me, and my stomach flooded with nausea. I was unable to move or speak.

A hand was applied to my mouth before the tall figure lifted me from the bed and carried me with ease out of my bedroom, along the hall, down the stairs, and into a room where I was plunged into darkness. The air was cold and smelt damp. Instead of a pillow my head rested against something hard and sterile. Bright beams of light forced my eyes shut tight against it.

The Shadow Man walked the length of the room, moving equipment, collecting and depositing instruments, before turning his attention to me, the girl who lay on her back on a hospital bed, legs raised in stirrups, tied apart.

The abduction scenario was as ancient as my insomnia. For years I had no idea who The Shadow Man was, but when I awoke, drenched in sweat and panting with terror – whether I'd invented it or I'd truly remembered something – I pictured my father stood over me as I attempted to wrench my wrists free of the leather straps he'd restrained me with.

No matter how hard I pulled or how loud I screamed for help there was no way I was getting out of there before he'd done whatever it was that he wanted to me. I had no idea where I was, if my mother could hear me from the cold soundproofed room, if anyone would save me.

He moved toward me, his face as hard as stone. His usually gruff voice sinisterly hypnotic. 'Carys.'

*

'Carys!'

I jolted awake. My eyes snapped open. My skin was slick with sweat, my hair was so wet it stuck to my face.

Lewis was leaning over me, hands on my shoulders, the pressure of his touch and the memory of my nightmare converging, sliding across my eyelids, bringing a fresh feral scream from my mouth which pierced through the silence.

'Shush, it's okay.'

Once my panic had subsided and my breathing normalized, Lewis released me, and I felt once again incredibly alone and scared.

'Another bad dream, huh?'

I nodded, unable to meet his eyes.

'I haven't been sleeping all that well either,' he admitted. 'I can't help thinking about those poor girls. You must be devastated. I can't imagine finding all this out about your own-'

'Stop it.'

Lewis looked down at his lap. 'I know this is hard for you-'

'I don't want to discuss this shit anymore. I've had enough.'

I clambered from the bed, ripping the duvet away from my feet where it was bundled, legs trembling, hands fumbling around in the dark. When I switched on the light the click dislodged something in my brain. Something ugly and awful. My heart pounded as I tried to blink it away.

'Hey, where are you going? It's 3:00am.'

I threw off my pyjamas and hurried into a pair of jeans, a vest top and a sweater. I stabbed my feet into my trainers and grabbed the key to the car from Lewis' coat that was hung over the back of the chair beside the window. I looked out into the mauve sky, a light drizzling of mist blanketing my view of the road.

'Carys?'

'I can't sleep. I'm going for a drive.'

The boys would fall asleep after a long drive when they were still unaccustomed to my need for rest after unbroken sleep caused by night feeds and endless months of teething. Maybe it would help me with this too.

I ignored Lewis' concern, assessing the risk of allowing me to roam alone in an area I didn't know all that well, at the time of night when nightclubbers were returning home drunk and impulsive. He stood slightly delirious at the door and hissed at me not to go, to return to bed. But I ignored his warning and tread softly down the corridor, crept down the carpeted staircase, and through the front door to meet the whistling wind.

I drove on autopilot, coming into awareness as though from a trance as I parked up outside the farm.

It looked different with blue and white tape flapping about in the gale. Two police cars were parked up at the end of the lane just a few yards ahead. I sat in the car a while, got out and walked around to ease my stiff limbs, then stood and stared at the clumps of earth decorating the lawn that had been dug up beneath a blood-red pre-dawn sky.

I turned at the sound of keys jangling to find a small Yorkshire Terrier bounding through the puddles. He left mucky footprints across my shoes and climbed my trouser leg for a stroke.

Gwenda appeared, turning the corner toward the farm. Her fiery red hair matching her blushed-from-exertion face beneath the sliver of moonlight that splintered through the bunched-up clouds overhead. She panted a greeting, looking worn thin. I assumed the dog had run off, that she'd been chasing after it.

'There you are,' she bent to retrieve him, holding the dog against her bust like a baby while she tried to catch her breath.

I blinked away the image of the baby's bones I'd found just a few days before and caught the look of sympathy that swept across her face.

'I don't expect you're up this early for a morning jog?'

'I couldn't sleep.'

'Me neither. All this business with . . . well, you look like you could do with a coffee.'

I should have thanked her for the offer, sensing she wanted to talk, but self-absorbed and unsure how anyone could miss the signs the person you saw daily was a serial killer, I felt nothing but hostility toward her. 'Did you know, what my father did?'

She bit her lip. 'Why don't we go back to mine, it's not far? Then we can get some caffeine down our necks and have a chat.'

I followed her down the track, away from the watchful eyes of the police officer who had left his station at the front door unguarded to walk to the end of the lane to inspect our movements. Our voices in the dead quiet must have alerted him to our presence.

The dog certainly hadn't.

Whether the police officer recognised me or not I couldn't tell and didn't care. I was fed up with everyone treading on eggshells around me. I was a grown woman. I didn't need the hard truth to be wrapped up in soft lace. I didn't want people to patronize me with gentle words or offer me a pity party for having a murderous father. I felt that Gwenda with her bold, brash personality understood that, and so I accepted her offer of a coffee, looking forward to getting out of the cold.

We walked through the pitch darkness, feet squelching in puddles to reach the house where Gwenda lived with her Yorkie, Shadow. 'He follows me everywhere,' she said.

The word *shadow* hummed in my ears long enough for me to register where I'd heard it from and in what context other than the fact that I called the strange man who visited me at night The Shadow Man.

'She's your little shadow, Bryn,' my mother said smiling, as I looked down at the girl from the top right-hand corner of the room, as though my soul had escaped my body and floated up to the ceiling to view the scene of myself from a third-person perspective.

I swallowed a wave of sickness.

The memory must have been recently implanted because I knew I had none. Certainly not at that age.

I entered the lounge with its rustic, old-world interior and noted the stuffed shelves of books lining the room. The lightly dust-coated animal ornaments, and the dog, Shadow's, belongings which took up far more of the room than Iefan or Rhys' toys ever had when they were younger. Perhaps my father wasn't the only person who liked to hoard things. Perhaps it was an age thing, or something lonely people did.

*Is that why your father collected girls, do you think?* The voice, mine, whispered into my ear as Gwenda handed me a boiling cup of coffee that I couldn't remember witnessing her pour or stir as we stood in the kitchen beside an oval pinewood table. She pulled out a dining chair and waited for me to sit before doing the same and taking a long, loud sip of her coffee.

It was almost 6:00am. I'd left my mobile phone in the B&B. I'd been gone for three hours. Lewis would be going out of his mind wondering where I was, or if he'd managed to sleep at all expecting to wake up beside me, to go downstairs for a fry-up together as soon as Good Morning Britain finished.

'How long have you known my father?'

'Two years I worked for him. I did the cleaning to begin with, then the regular housework, shopping, and helped him pay the bills. He was never very polite on the phone and hated all the waiting around and pressing buttons to speak to an automated voice recording. *Bastard robots taking over the world*, he said.'

I almost smiled. That sounded like my father.

But what she said next didn't. Weren't ancient leopards too old to change their spots?

'He regretted not trying harder to contact you, so I sought you out. You weren't difficult to find, what with the photography website and everything. But I didn't tell him. I thought you must have decided against contact for good reason.' She gave me a look that suggested she suspected just what that reason was, but she continued talking so I was excused from having to comment on my behaviour. Not that I felt I should have to explain my decision to avoid contact with my father, just that I knew she expected me to.

'I think he wanted the company more than

anything. I didn't help him with anything he wasn't able to do himself.'

Narcissistic. Manipulative. That sounded more like the father I knew.

'When did he get ill?'

'Ah,' she said. 'The heart attack. Well, he had angina, so his death wasn't entirely unexpected. But that wasn't what killed him.'

She paused for effect, and the room began to spin, the world tilting on its axis. She lowered her voice. 'Divine intervention helped him along.'

I almost dropped the cup when Gwenda spoke again, convinced I'd misheard her, asking her to repeat herself, my voice hoarse from lack of sleep, hand shaking, my grip tightening around the china cup that wobbled before turning and slopping the caramel coloured liquid onto the burgundy carpet.

'It was bound to happen sooner or later.'

'Are you insinuating someone assisted him to his death?'

The only conceivable conclusion to glean from Gwenda's metaphorical message was that *she* had eased my father toward the departure lounge of this world. Because from what I gathered she was the only person he'd allowed into his life, his home, in two decades.

'What dear?'

'You're saying he was murdered?'

'I'm sorry I . . .' She took her full cup of coffee to the sink and poured the hot liquid into the steel abyss.

I followed her to the cupboard where she stood staring at a tower of tins, mostly peas, before bringing one out to place into the fridge, seemingly forgetting what task she was to perform next.

It was frightening how oddly childlike she appeared in that moment. I placed a hand on her shoulder to rouse her from her trance. 'My father, you said he was killed.'

'Did I?' She turned to me, face confused.

'You did.' I waited for a response, but none was forthcoming. Then she retrieved a pack of sausages from the fridge, removed their wrapping and set them on a plate, uncooked.

She heard the soles of my trainers squeak on the seventies-style, patterned brown linoleum, and said, 'I'm sorry, but who are you and what are you doing in my house?'

'You invited me in.'

'I don't think so. Out. Or I'll call the police.' She pointed to the back door that led out onto a lush green lawn, surrounded by shrubs and potted begonias, visible through the leaded glass.

'Gwenda, do you not remember me?'

'No. Should I?'

'Yes, you worked for my father, Bryn Howell.'

'That man is not welcome here.'

'He passed away,' I said incredulously.

'Good riddance to him,' she spat. Then she looked up at me, face seething with barely restrained rage and said, 'ah hah, you're his daughter. The photographer,' and smiled, pleased her memory had returned.

'That's right.'

'Would you like a cup of coffee?'

'Uh, please.'

She set about boiling the kettle to pour us both another coffee. All the while my mind was whirring like a washing machine. As I watched her movements and listened to her repeatedly state her displeasure toward the modern biscuit packaging that confused her and my father's bad manners, I realized she was suffering some form of dementia.

Poor cow, I thought. Wouldn't it be awful to find yourself trapped in groundhog-day for the rest of your years?

Then I thought that was exactly how Ella must have felt, waking to the same routine day-in day-out, wherever she was kept, until my father had enough of her and decided to put an end to her miserable life.

# BRYN

*Brynmawr, Ebbw Vale, Wales, 1998*

Siân's mother pleaded with the camera for her daughter's safe return. Lyn's red hair and dazzling green eyes were inherited from her father's Irish Catholic genealogy, or so the press liked to play on. As though the fact her Romany gypsy ancestry somehow made her grating voice more charming to viewers because she was religious.

'She should have been watching her daughter better, bloody pikey,' whispered the men down the pub.

'Siân if you're watching this and you can, please come home. If somebody has taken you against your will, know that I love you and I'm doing my very best to find you. If you have her, let her go.'

Her voice cracked, and she broke down just before

Bryn switched off the television and left the living room to fetch a bottle of water and a cheese sandwich which he took with him down the hall, unlocking the door to the basement, switching on the light, and closing the door behind him before descending the steps.

He heard Carys' footsteps bounding down the hall above him as he lay the plated meal down onto the single wooden chair in one corner, which was angled to face the room. He glanced back at the mattress on the concrete floor and what was on it, then marched back upstairs, slamming the door behind him. He dropped the key in his haste to get as far away from the basement as quickly as possible.

Something below their feet thudded. Carys, a cup in hand, on her way to the kitchen, stood in the hall eying him warily.

'Must be the ironing board I just used falling over.' He didn't want her to wonder why he kept returning to the door he'd told her just led to a broom cupboard.

She gave him a strange look, then bolted up to her room. It wasn't long before he heard loud thudding music coming from behind her locked bedroom door.

The bass drowned out the sounds excreted from the basement.

He doubted she could recall visiting the room when she was small, but he brought Carys down there too. They used to watch films together when Rhiannon couldn't stand the noise of a television unless *Only Fools and Horses* was on. It was the only programme she'd watch. She begged him to get rid of the television once she'd decided it was an unhealthy pastime, but he was adamant her fear of technology was unnecessary.

She placed Jehovah on a pedestal and devoured his word, forsaking her family's desires for those of the preachers' whose pointless religion she had adopted commanded.

Carys was a terrible sleeper, suffered nightmares throughout her early years so sometimes Bryn brought her downstairs, so her cries wouldn't be heard from her tearful, migraine-inflected, apoplectic mother. As time wore on it became a regular occurrence so he brought the chair down from the kitchen to sit on while he read to her. Next came the mattress so if she fell asleep, she could stay there. He left the door ajar in case she awoke during the night needing the toilet. He didn't enjoy having to mop up her mess in the morning. The mattress stank, was already soiled, but he wiped it as best as he could manage without the housework queen's help. There were times he had to teach Carys a lesson when her bed-wetting got out of control, but rather than help it hindered the message he was attempting to convey so after a while he left her wrapped up in the sodden sheets. The cold stale urine providing a greater punishment.

He wasn't ashamed to have inherited his fathers use of discipline in his own household, but he didn't want Rhiannon to walk in on him while he was dispensing it. It was a private matter, between him and his daughter, and Rhiannon's opinion on the subject was of no concern to him.

What he *was* afraid of though, was the escalation of his unholy thoughts when he was alone with his daughter and shut off from his wife's watchful gaze. That was something he still didn't understand, and he didn't think anyone else would either.

# CARYS

*Redland, Bristol, England, 2004*

Iefan ran from Lewis' arms and into mine as I lay in the hospital bed, the scent of disinfectant and the clean white sheets reminding me of something that in my sleepy daze I could not recover.

The maternity ward was filled with the sound of crying babies, the soles of shoes slapping against the squeaky linoleum, and hurried conversations as midwives scrambled down the corridor to deliver another small child. I looked down at the one I cradled in my arms, disbelieving for a second that he was mine.

Rhys shared his father's eye colour, his large nose and wide eyebrows. But while Iefan stroked his new-born brother's hand, I stared at his eyes, and saw my father in them.

At age four, Iefan was a typical boy, bounding down the stairs, jumping the final five, climbing over the sofa, drawing on walls with non-toxic crayon that couldn't be wiped from the matt paint, and filling the toilet with his beloved toys. I called him my little tornado. When I looked at him it was as though I was staring at the eye of a storm. But I wouldn't have it any other way. Which was why, when I returned home the following morning with a new-born Rhys bundled up inside his car seat and I was suddenly plunged into a darkness I could see no way of escaping, feeling the universe shift as though the parallels between the past and present were attempting to merge, I did not say anything. I feared being labelled a bad mother, a depressive. Both terms suggested a vulnerability in me, a weakness I didn't want to acknowledge. So I put up with feeling distanced from my infant son and suffered in silence.

The nightmares began the night we brought Rhys home. Along with the constant sense of doom and the foreboding atmosphere that seemed to follow me around the house. For years I felt as if a shadow was cast above me, and my sleep was destroyed.

Lewis asked me once when Rhys was small, if I

knew why his birth had been particularly traumatic for me. I assured him it was no worse than Iefan's, but I could not ignore the crushing panic that fell over me in waves as I lay vulnerable, exposed in that hospital bed.

I felt The Shadow Man's presence. At one point during labour I even thought I'd seen him. Perhaps the white plastic bed, stirrups, smell of disinfectant, steel cabinet, and blindingly bright overhanging light had dislodged the memories. But it was a difficult thing to explain to my midwife, and then health visitor upon my return home, so I kept the concern from my voice when she came to weigh Rhys and check on my stitches, tried to put it to the back of my mind.

I looked up the phenomenon online. The Shadow Man appeared throughout the world, tormenting people from their peripheral vision, appearing in the darkness as they lay in their beds, or in dreams. Psychologists believed he was the representation of our outer selves. Spiritualists said he was a guardian. Scientists suggested he was a trick of the light. And neurologists argued it was a symptom of frontal lobe disturbance caused by a cognitive dysfunction within the brain.

I never thought it strange I had no memory of my childhood. I assumed it was normal. I heard somewhere that we don't store or retrieve memories until we turn three or four years old and can't recall them with any accuracy until we reach six years of age. But mine began the day Seren went missing.

Was her disappearance significant? Or was it just because we were the same age: twelve years old, when she vanished?

I didn't know and wasn't sure I wanted to find out, so I continued to suffer the abductions each night, worried that if I told Lewis he'd think I was crazy. I didn't want to hear the words my mother used to explain away the things I said or the socially unacceptable way I apparently behaved around strange men. Though I had no recollection, she reminded me often enough how abnormal I was.

In my dreams I was a child. But when I awoke, I could not remember anything before the day our quiet little town, became one of the most popular in the country while it seemed every nearby police force flocked to Ebbw Vale in search of Seren Lloyd.

I wanted to unearth a reason for the nightmares. I

wanted to know why, aside from the haunting visions my mother suggested were demonic forces attempting to lure me toward Satan, I'd been chosen for the nightly visitations.

I visited the library and read up on alien abductions. The cases were fascinating, and I identified with almost everything the victims recalled. But I still had a hard time convincing myself I should come clean and speak to someone about it. Who would believe me?

My mother had tried for years to drill into me that I was a fantasist and that I imagined things. But why was it that I could remember the abductions and the medical experiments, but could not recall one celebration, one day trip, one school play, nothing before I turned twelve?

Was Iefan's age significant in that the time my nightmares began he was two years below the age at which I appeared in them?

Had something happened to me, back then, when I was a six-year-old girl?

Or had The Shadow Man erased my childhood memories, wiped them clean during one of my abductions?

I laughed aloud. The idea was preposterous, but what other explanation could there be?

# BRYN

*Brynmawr, Ebbw Vale, Wales, 2018*

Gwenda arrived five minutes early wearing her usual eccentric style of fabrics. Not one to adhere to the dress-code of a sixty-odd-year-old woman her emerald green headscarf wrapped around her bright red locks, large gold earrings and jazzy blue and yellow summer dress made her look like she'd just stepped off the platform of a Vogue catwalk in 1988.

Her green eyes lit up at the sight of two crisp twenty-pound notes lying on the table beside the phone that never rang.

'Quit moping around and get out there,' she said, retrieving the money he owed her for doing his shopping the morning before. 'The sun won't last forever. Rain's been forecast for the rest of the week.'

Nobody else would have got away with speaking to

Bryn the way she did, but her words compelled him to listen. He dragged his carcass from the chair and despite the pain in his gnarled bones he tugged open the heavy wooden front door that expanded in the heat and stepped out into the glorious sunshine.

The day Gwenda arrived at the newly bought property neighbouring his with her Yorkshire Terrier in arm they'd quite literally bumped into each other, got talking, and Bryn had accepted her kind offer to buy his groceries. His arthritis was getting worse and having lived alone for two decades he'd started to see the benefits that a lodger might bring. But Gwenda living merely a quarter of a mile away meant he didn't need to concern himself with strangers rooting through his things or checking up on the whereabouts of the individual he lived with in case they came across something on the farm he didn't want them to see. If Gwenda did the chores for him, it would mean she could return home each day. And she didn't bother asking him about his dead wife or estranged daughter.

'Don't I know you?' he said, a spark of recognition igniting then fizzling out when he couldn't remember from where he'd seen her before.

'I'm not from around here.'

Gwenda was a hard-faced woman who got things done. And that was why after she'd collected then delivered the groceries for him on that July morning, putting them away to save him the job and offering to do his cleaning too, he hadn't thought twice about accepting. 'Just until you get back on your feet,' she said.

'I'll have to pay you.'

'Nonsense. That's what neighbours are for.'

But nobody worked for free unless they wanted something in return, and he was adamant he would pay her to ensure she didn't ask for a favour in the future. 'Fine. We'll work out a rate later.'

It was only supposed to be a short-term arrangement, but he'd kept her on, finding more things for her to do that he could no longer be bothered to do himself. Besides, it was nice having a female around the house again.

So, that day, the same as every other, she made him a cup of tea, handed him his vitamin pills, and watched to ensure he swallowed them before she started on the housework.

Gwenda was a stickler for healthy living and a tidy

home. And when she'd finished washing the dishes of her own accord, she took his shopping list and left with the promise to check in on him that evening. 'I'll bring you round some of that broccoli and stilton soup I made yesterday.'

'Lovely. Thank you.' Her soup, always including a decent portion of Irish soda bread, was the best he'd ever tasted.

Two weeks ago, he'd had a fall. Not a bad one. Not like old Mrs Roylen from the post office he hadn't visited to collect his pension from since Gwenda offered to do it for him. Mrs Roylen had broken her ankle and fractured her front teeth as she fell down the steep stone steps to her bungalow. After requesting help from the council to be rehoused into a property without a staircase and securing financial assistance to install a wet room and downstairs toilet she'd sadly, ironically, injured herself *entering* the property.

Bryn's fall though was caused by a temporary loss of balance. Something he suffered from most mornings, along with vision disturbances. Sometimes he was positive he saw Rhiannon watching him from the doorway or heard noises from the empty basement he secretly thought was haunted by the girl who'd died in there. By midday he typically felt fine.

Were Rhiannon alive she would have thought the rats that were never present in the basement to begin with had returned, but Gwenda couldn't see or hear the things he did, so he feared that perhaps they were in his head and that it would be best if he kept the visions and the noises to himself, fearing madness was his comeuppance for what he'd done.

He knew now that it was wrong. He'd had time to self-evaluate. Years in fact. But back then, the rose-tinted nineties, his desires were all-consuming. The urge, the compulsion, was uncontrollable. It wasn't a crime. The girls weren't victims.

His father beat him as a child. It never did him any harm. He was far less heavy-handed with his own daughter. He understood now that what was acceptable back then is no more, but he never intended to gain pleasure from hurting Carys. It was something that just happened. A physiological response he couldn't prevent. And when she inquired as to why he felt the need to press his body against hers and hold her while she sobbed afterwards, he told her it was what all fathers did. And she believed him.

'What are you doing by the barn, Bryn?' Gwenda's voice forced him to stop.

He spun round and caught Gwenda's accusing sneer. He looked down at the soil and realised he was stood over the baby's grave. Ella's baby. His daughter. She'd have been twenty-two this year if she'd have lived. So sad, he thought, that life could be taken from you before you had even begun to live it.

At such a young age, Ella, the baby's mother, had the entire world at her feet. Now her twelve-year-old body was preserved below the ground beneath where he stood, having died shortly after the birth of their child.

He named the infant Branwen.

She was angelic, and her thick dark hair meant the name Beautiful Raven fit her aptly.

It was a shame she had to die.

# CARYS

*Redland, Bristol, England, 2012*

Iefan's fourteenth birthday party triggered something within me. My breath caught in my throat and I almost choked on a cocktail stick of cheese and pineapple, the odd combination of sweet and savoury buffet food I must have subconsciously inherited an enjoyment of because I'd enjoyed eating it at a party.

No, I thought. That can't be right. We didn't celebrate Christmas. Because according to my mother, Jehovah was born sometime between mid-September to the end of November. The time people generally associate with Christmas was in fact the winter solstice. The 25th of December was an Anglican movement to reinvent the pagan holiday. Christmas was a sacrilegious ritual she refused to acknowledge should have any part in our lives. So why did she allow me to attend Zoe's fourteenth birthday party in celebration of her Jewish coming of age?

Perhaps she felt bad for not providing me with any siblings, knowing I rarely had anyone to hang out with. Or maybe she just wanted to get me away from the farm.

My father had always felt unnaturally toward me. But the night he dropped me off at the party, the way he appraised Zoe, his eyes roaming back to me and locking eyes on mine as though pleading me not to let him down, to remain untouched by fumbling teenage hands, sealed it. I knew with certainty that his unhealthy appetite for disciplining me was a cloak used to cover a deeper, darker desire.

I didn't notice his car, the engine quiet beneath the backdrop of pop music emanating from the house as I stood on the front step waiting for him to arrive to collect me. My father's vehicle parked a safe enough distance away from the door so that I couldn't witness his face which I imagined must have worn a mixture of disgust and envy, until I'd entered it. His cheeks were flooded with colour and his knuckles were white on the steering wheel as he drove me home, consumed with a rage I couldn't comprehend.

He parked several yards away from the turning onto the lane that led to the house, so that my mother couldn't hear him berate me for allowing an immature, inexperienced boy to stick his tongue down my throat after he'd caught us sharing a goodbye kiss at the door. At the time I was mortified he'd seen us, then it dawned on me that what he felt wasn't something he should have.

'You're jealous,' I laughed.

His face twisted in fury, eyes dilated like a savage, and he lunged for me. 'I don't want my daughter to defile herself,' he spat, clenching my hair in his fists.

He tugged on it, forcing my head back, and when he dragged his hands away he ripped out chunks of it and it fell like confetti from between his fingers, decorating the black seats. 'You're mine. Nobody else's. Do you hear?'

I tried to fight him off. I lashed out, hands swiping at him, legs kicking, but it was no good. His muscled workman arms, farming hands, chiselled torso, too strong. I struggled and begged but could not evade the intent that burned like fire in his eyes.

When it was over, I felt sullied and ashamed. And I knew, in that moment, it was always going to happen.

It was my destiny. I was meant to lose my virginity to my father.

I wrenched open the bathroom door and bent over the toilet bowl, retching and shuddering with tears streaming down my face at the memory of it. I threw up just as I had the morning that I'd taken the pregnancy test, at sixteen years of age, two years after that first time in the car.

I'd bought the test in a Cardiff chemist, and bunked off school to pee on a stick in the filthy, stinking, public toilet of the train station where a junkie had passed out with a needle poking out of her arm. That's where I was when I discovered I was growing my father's baby inside my womb.

I'd bled intermittently during those first few weeks and considered the possibility I might lose the baby, but my stomach continued to grow.

I must have heard something about it on the television, because I convinced myself that what we'd done was incest and grew paranoid that our secret would get out and the illicit action meant I was a criminal, that I would be sent to prison. I feared the day the police would come knocking on the door to charge me. The only option I had, I thought, was to leave Ebbw Vale and get as far away from my father as quickly as possible. But I couldn't do it alone. My baby needed a father.

I had to give the infant that shared far too much of my familial DNA a proper family, like the one I never had, if he or she had any hope of a normal life.

The chance came a couple of weeks later in the form of a tall, handsome gentleman called Lewis.

He had a job, a car, and was unafraid of fatherhood when I told him he'd got me pregnant. We'd only slept together once, but we both knew that was all it took.

He never questioned why Iefan was born four weeks premature. 'He's a good size for thirty-six weeks gestation,' said the midwife. And he didn't seem to notice Iefan's features were closer to my fathers than his.

I heard later, as Iefan began to grow, that children born from incestuous relationships suffered birth defects, but Iefan was perfect.

It took Zoe's birthday party to accept that the way my father acted toward me was abnormal.

Bryn had groomed me from a young age, distancing me from my mother and showering me with gifts for keeping secrets. I came to understand that the deception was a way to keep me in line and a test to see how far he could push me, how willing I was to go the extra distance to withhold things from my mother, my peers, my teachers, and Bill Erwin so that nobody would ever find out what my father had been doing to me behind my locked bedroom door as he read me those bedtime stories.

I looked across the room, watching Iefan move a pen along the page of his notepad as he drew a skull for his art project and another memory slammed against me like a physical object had struck me in the chest.

The vision of a twelve-year-old me, my small hand gripped around a bright blue pen with a fluffy yellow top, pressing the ink hard onto a lined page as I sat with my knees raised up to my chest beneath the duvet of my single bed. The light from the torch lying on the mattress aimed at my childish scrawl.

My diary. Where was it?

Could it still be in the house where my father remained alone and growing old?

I imagined it stuffed at the bottom of a box somewhere amongst the accumulation of school paintings, my first pair of knitted booties, and the photograph albums my father kept closeted in the attic.

Was it possible he'd found it?

A wave of sickness rose to my throat.

Had he read it?

Iefan put the pencil down and began to shade in the 3D chair he'd drawn, effecting a shadow by smudging the grey pencil marks with his finger. He collected a green pencil to work in the reflected light of the glossy cushioned seat, and an ice-cold chill coated my skin.

It was the same shade of green as the dress Seren Lloyd was wearing the day she vanished.

I remembered the argument between my mother and father about his light blue car, stolen within hours of her disappearance.

Had my father chosen not to punish me for telling my mother I'd witnessed his car – recognising the number plate – as it swerved the corner of Castle Lane because it would prove he'd been driving it after he claimed it was stolen, and he was frightened the police would find out? Or to protect me from explaining to my mother why I was late home the afternoon that Seren went missing?

My mother suggested the school-girl I'd seen wearing the emerald green dress on her way to her dance lesson wasn't Seren, but how would I have known what she was wearing before her disappearance was reported on the news that evening if I had misidentified her?

I wasn't supposed to have been walking home alone from school that day, but my father hadn't come to collect me. Rather than wait until he arrived I travelled the mile-long journey thinking I could catch up with Zoe. We separated when we reached the junction a few short metres from Glynis Owens' grocery shop.

My father used it as leverage, threatening to inform my mother I'd run off, but he never told me why he hadn't met me outside the school gates and I often wondered what he'd been up to. Or if he knew where I was or who with, and that was why he'd lied about my late arrival home.

# BRYN

*Brynmawr, Ebbw Vale, Wales, 2018*

Gwenda's dementia was getting worse. There was no doubt that in a year or less, she would forget to drop by, and Bryn would be left without food or his pension. Some mornings she forgot to hand over his pills, and others she bought two lots of groceries, always forgetting the milk. His health was deteriorating too, and he was worried his GP, who visited once a month to check his blood pressure, would refer him to the care home as he'd previously advised so that there would always be someone to keep a close eye on him. Bryn had refused the room after his fall but without family or friends to rely on to support his decision his future might one day be in the state's hands.

Bill Erwin was no longer around. He'd visited

often after the death of his wife, but as time had worn on, he'd moved forward, had found a female companion to fill her place. When he'd been diagnosed with cancer, Bryn had taken on the role of supporting him through it, as he had done for Bryn after Rhiannon had died. But Bill considered his illness justice for sins unknown, choosing to spend his days absorbed in Jehovah's writings, visited only by members of his cult. He often wondered what it must have been like for Bill to know that when he died, he would leave no legacy.

'Gwenda?'

'Yes, Bryn?'

'Do you have a family?'

A shadow fell over her face. She looked like she was absorbed in a distant and dark memory. 'No. I've never been married, and I don't have children.'

They'd never shared such intimacies before. Gwenda was guarded and Bryn disliked people poking their noses in. Until that day their friendship had been purely professional. He'd discovered from her reply what he'd hoped to, though there were still issues unattended they could wait.

He sat forward, removed the envelope from

behind the cushion at his back and handed it to her. 'I need you to post this. It's important.'

She glanced at the address for the solicitors in town then deposited it in her handbag. She offered Bryn a tight smile.

Could he trust her, this woman who'd appeared from nowhere, befriended him, gladly taken a key to access his property, and without once appearing put out or annoyed had graced him with her presence on lonely stormy nights, helped him when he was in need, and never asked for anything in return?

Although he paid her, she seemed to accept the notes reluctantly.

His father's words came back to haunt him. 'Nobody ever does anything for anyone for nothing, son.'

He watched Gwenda eyeing the photographs mounted on the wall. Long ago memories threatened to resurface so he quashed them.

'You alright, love? Here,' he pointed to the sofa. 'Sit down. Your wandering is making my head spin.'

'Sorry, what?'

She looked confused. The short-term memory loss was evident in her eyes. Sometimes he wondered if she recognised him, and others her face wore a scowl and he wondered if perhaps she could read his thoughts.

Her face was instantly recognisable the day he'd bumped into her in the lane, but he couldn't lay claim to reason why. She'd lived miles from the farm, she said. Had grown up in Abergavenny and had taken a nursing post in Gloucestershire Royal hospital. Her retirement left her lonely and feeling isolated, so she moved to Ebbw Vale.

He asked her once, what drew her to the picturesque landscape he'd only ever known.

'The valleys contain my soul Bryn,' she'd said.

But he wondered if that was all.

She'd mentioned once that she'd been born in Gaelic lands, not Celtic ones, not that there was any need. Her accent grew stronger when she was in a low mood.

The post fell through the door, late as usual. Sometimes the postman didn't bother to come at all, in rain or high winds. Bryn supposed he kept the post for days until there was too much cluttering up the house he shared with his young son since his girlfriend had walked out on them and delivered a weeks-worth in one go. Or maybe it was Bryn's paranoia that led him to suspect everyone of wrongdoing.

Gwenda left her seat vacant to collect the bills and leaflets advertising pizza takeaways, doorstep loans, and conservatory installation at a twenty percent discount. She dropped the post on his lap and went for the door.

'Aren't you forgetting something?' He pointed downward to where her handbag lay on the floor at his feet, noting the distinctive NHS issued brown bottle of some unknown pills that were half disguised beneath her purse.

She collected it from the carpet and spun round to face him. 'I'll come back later,' she said.

He followed her move down the hall and out the front door. Then he glanced up to the photograph that hung on the wall to his left. The one Gwenda had been looking at. His daughter's teenage eyes stared back at him.

'Where are you, Carys? Where is our child?' he said once he heard the front door slam closed in the wind.

He hoped Carys had given their kid a good life.

After the initial heartbreak of losing them both,

he'd grown envious of them. Branwen hadn't survived.

He'd planned on returning Ella to the roadside where he'd picked her up from, but her pregnancy forced him to alter his plan.

Ella James died in the basement, just hours after the death of their daughter, ten months after her disappearance. And the only thing left for him to do was cover their bodies up, pretend he wasn't responsible, and pray nobody ever found out where they were buried.

# CARYS

*Brynmawr, Ebbw Vale, Wales, 2018*

I hadn't yet read the county coroner's post-mortem report regarding my father's death. I was so all-consumed with the resulting panic of returning to Wales and loading up Bryn's stuff to throw away, so I could sell the property – no siblings meant the probate service went through without protest or long-drawn-out negotiations – I hadn't before had time to bother looking through the ins and outs of how he'd died. Then I'd discovered the skull and it didn't seem important. But after what Gwenda had implied during our brief conversation at her house before she'd forgotten who I was and why I was there, I'd decided to study it, questioning whether there was any truth in what she'd said.

His cause of death clearly stated: Medical; Heart

failure. But according to his health records his angina was a recent phenomenon. Hadn't Gwenda said he suffered from high blood pressure which caused his angina, that led to his continued monthly home visits from his concerned GP?

I'd spoken to Gwenda over the phone, and discovered she was a nurse for thirty-five years, qualifying in 1981. After leaving Abergavenny in 1998 she'd continued her career in Gloucester. 'That's why your father employed me,' she said. 'Because of my experience.'

I made a note to chase down her details and dig further.

The internet was a prime source of information for me, and most of my recent knowledge came from the many websites dedicated to facial reconstruction and bone deterioration. According to one article written by a specialist in the field, baby's bones were far too dense to provide a definitive reason for their death but the minerals within Ella's offered the pathologist a clue as to how she may have died. It turned out my theory wasn't far wrong. She'd likely died during childbirth. Placental material was discovered embedded onto her extended pubis bone, suggesting the placenta hadn't been fully expelled. I learned this caused internal bleeding and infection. The baby had possibly died either shortly before or during birth, strangled by the umbilical cord. Childbirth was Ella's killer, but my father was the cause of her pregnancy, so as far as I was concerned, he'd contributed to both of their deaths.

DI Locke and her colleague kept me up to date with their findings, but the detectives were not holding out hope that Seren or Siân were still alive.

Our conversation that morning resulted in my lunch time launch into Costa, while Lewis and the boys played golf. It was seated in the warm bustling café after DI Locke had departed that I uncovered more about the elusive Gwenda, whose surname I rolled round on my tongue, wondering if it was mere coincidence and praying the detectives had already questioned her about it. Her surname was Kavanagh.

Gwenda worked as a part time carer for my father for two solid years before his heart failed and ceased its rhythmic beat. If she were alive when my mother was, I had no doubt from her no-nonsense attitude she would have insisted Rhiannon took her medication, just as she had with my father.

There were so many pills left-over after my mother's death I was positive they hadn't all been packed away and stored in my old bedroom, the one I imagined had been turned into a shrine for my mother's belongings after I'd left home, never intending to return. But I found no evidence she'd existed at all when I'd checked during the two hours we had to declutter before I'd found the infants remains and Lewis had called the police.

I knew he'd die someday, but I thought Bryn's death would cause me to feel guilty for leaving him to die alone. But he hadn't. Gwenda had been there, had watched him suck his final breath.

No, that wasn't right. My mind was playing tricks on me. I read the sentence of the post-mortem report again, disbelieving it for a moment.

Gwenda told me on the phone, calling the number she'd found on my professional photography website four months prior, that she'd found my father deceased in his armchair, that the coroner had recorded his death as heart failure. But according to the report, Gwenda was seated on the sofa opposite, watched him clutch his chest and die. She'd told the police the same thing. Yet the story she gave me was out of sync. A heart attack or cardiac failure as the inquest stated was written nine days after Gwenda had found him. She'd contacted me to break the news of his death six days before it was written. So how had she known what the lab's report implied before the post-mortem examination had been conducted?

Unless she had been there.

Heart attacks were sometimes obvious, so it was possible she'd witnessed his death and concluded by professional experience what had caused him to die. So why had she lied to me and said she'd found him lifeless, cold, and rigid in his armchair three days after he'd died?

The thought of Gwenda witnessing my father's demise would strangely have comforted me. Did she not want me to know she'd been in the house at the time of his death, somehow sensing my disdain for the old man? Or had she a more sinister motive for keeping me in the dark?

*Death swallows those he knows must be returned to Jehovah*, my mother's words rang through my head.

Rhiannon refused to take her medication and wouldn't have been pleased if my father had been prescribed anything, considering ill health God's will.

She spurned insulin, disbelieving in messing with nature, after years of profitable brainwashing tactics by the elder of her religious sect.

Gwenda told me she had studiously ensured Bryn pop the vitamin pills there was no record of his GP ordering him to take or having prescribed, after quitting her job in nursing to care for my elderly father. What did those pills contain? Why hadn't the police discovered the empty boxes amongst the crap left lying around the farm during their search?

Until the development of angina followed by his death two years later, Gwenda had been working in a hospital staffed by some of the leading cardiac specialists in the county. Was it an anomaly or coincidence that she covered cardiology before purchasing a property down the road from my father after retiring as a ward sister, working below the diabetic specialist under the post of unit leader after swapping her role in 2012?

I had no idea what relevance this had to my father's death except a creeping suspicion that began in my toes and worked its way up until lodging itself in my throat, forcing me to lean forward, choking on the possibility Gwenda might have planned to befriend my lonely old father for his money, killing him to ensure she got it.

Or was there another motive I had yet to establish?

And if my suspicions were proved correct, did it matter if she had?

The way he'd behaved while he was alive was sinful. He deserved to die.

# BRYN

*Brynmawr, Ebbw Vale, Wales, 2018*

Gwenda stared at him from across the room as though he'd spouted horns. She was angry and Bryn had no idea what had brought it about, or why she now thundered from the living room, across the hallway and began tugging on the door he'd told her was a broom cupboard, which really led down to the basement.

'Is this where you kept her?'

He didn't need to ask who, it was written in her eyes. Gwenda knew he'd disposed of the girl. He should have guessed Siân was her daughter. They shared the surname Kavanagh.

He had recognised her from the press conference; the mother begging for her missing daughter to return home. Perhaps deep in his subconscious he'd always known but had been denying it.

He was good at that.

'Answer me Bryn. I've waited so long for this. Just tell me where she's buried. I'm assuming she's still down there? Did you . . . did you pour concrete over her or-'

'I don't know what you're talking about.'

'Two years I've cleaned your underpants and slaved away for you, hoping, praying your conscience would one day rear some decency, but you continue to deny it, even to yourself.'

She stood there, facing him, hands on hips, demanding he tell her where he'd buried her daughter, but he couldn't, wouldn't divulge where the girl's resting place was. It wasn't healthy to drag up the past like this.

'Fetch some tea.'

She scowled at him. 'Tea? Fucking tea? My daughter, Bryn. You killed my daughter and you want me to make you tea. I'll boil the kettle and pour it on your fucking head!'

'Gwenda, I would never have hurt her. You must know that. I . . .' His mouth dried as he scrambled to find the words that he'd been practicing for years in case a situation such as this ever arose.

'Then who did, Bryn?'

He'd almost given away his deepest, darkest secret. He felt the shedding of the last of his armour slipping away as he spoke. 'I know who you are. Your Siân's mother, Lyn. Gwendalyn. You think I took your daughter.'

They were all facts, thrown at her. He waited for her reaction, his blood hot and roaring through his ears.

How had she found out? She couldn't know anything, not for certain. Or at least she hadn't until he'd opened his trapdoor of a mouth.

He expected her to grab the poker leant against the fireplace and lunge at him, strike him repeatedly over the head with it, but her face contorted and hot salty tears fell down her supple cheeks as she crumpled to the floor, her world imploding.

He should comfort her, apologise, reason why he'd done the awful things he had. But he didn't feel remorse, only hatred toward her.

Everything Gwenda had told him had been a lie. She'd befriended him and persuaded him to replace Carys' name on his will by pretending she didn't want his money thus making him feel sorry for her enough that he'd leave it to her. She'd cheated him out of his inheritance to cover the cost of his funeral plan, which would leave her with a vast amount after paying for it upon his death. She'd ironed his shirts, mopped the floor, and after gaining his trust had listened to him discuss the wife who'd died before him, who he loved dearly, and the daughter who'd walked out on him, who he felt nothing for. And all the while she'd been playing him for a fool.

He felt no pity for her. She deserved whatever fate served her for what she'd done, entering his house under false pretences, hiding her true intentions from him.

Gwenda was a liability. She had to go.

# CARYS

*Brynmawr, Ebbw Vale, Wales, 2018*

I couldn't believe I hadn't put two and two together earlier. I stared at the twenty-two-year-old newspaper clipping and it was immediately obvious. Gwenda was Siân's mother. She'd set a trap for my father. What I couldn't explain was why it had taken her two years to enact. Then it dawned on me. Being a nurse, she would have had access to patient records via the NHS, to medicine that could both save and end a person's life. If she'd done just that then why had she taken so long?

I trawled the internet for prescriptions that would cause angina symptoms. I came across various things, but two stuck. Insulin and beta-blockers. When taken together they cause disturbances in blood pressure and heart rate. It was a fast, inexpensive way to cause heart arrhythmia, tachycardia too, emulating a cardiac arrest. And I'd no doubt she had a vast supply of such medicines in my father's house from when my mother was sick. By the time Rhiannon had died his hoarding had got out of control. He never returned the unused prescriptions. That's why I couldn't find the bottles when I searched his home; she'd disposed of them.

I looked up the side-effects of taking insulin and made a list down one side of a sheet of A4, writing the symptoms of diabetes alongside them. They were almost identical. Nobody would suspect that someone suffering from palpitations or imbalanced blood pressure had ingested substances that caused it, not if they presented with symptoms of chest-tightness, nausea, breathlessness, and the occasional pain extending from neck and shoulder to ribs or vice versa, for so long. Two years was ample time for Gwenda's actions to convince Bryn and a small selection of medical professionals he had a problem with his heart.

I couldn't forget the fact Gwenda had inherited a substantial sum of money from him too, wasting no time in claiming fifteen thousand pounds from his estate. To convince a man to sign over that amount of cash would take a while. Two years it appeared. His funeral cost just two thousand pounds, which could easily have come from his pension, so a considerably comfortable amount of money would remain.

But was it blood money or compensation?

I knew withholding vital information from the police who were trying to help disclose my father's crimes was a criminal act. Obstruction of justice carried a maximum custodial sentence of ten years. 'Perjury,' my mother would have called it. But the last thing on my mind right then was snitching on a sixty-three-year-old woman. A woman who'd lost her daughter, future, and survived only on memories- bad ones, that she seemed to be losing. Like the day her daughter had disappeared. And whatever knowledge had led her to suspect my father of killing her.

I didn't think taking the law into her own spindly hands was right, and I didn't agree with the concept of an eye for an eye as laid out in the bible was the correct thing to do. Murder, whichever way it swings, for good or evil, was a sin. But what inner turmoil, what emotional pain, and inconsolable desolation had Gwenda felt when her daughter, Siân, had been snatched from the street and bundled into my father's car, awaiting a fate worse than death? A lengthy torturous existence before he disposed of her.

Where, when, or how I did not know.

The crushing guilt for choosing not to pass on to the detectives what I was aware of was almost unbearable. I knew I shouldn't, but suspecting she had dementia due to our previous meeting, I wished she'd forget she'd killed my father so if or when the police realised that she was responsible for assisting him to his death, her lack of guilt would be genuine, and they'd have nothing to base a charge on.

I was playing a dangerous game, one I knew I couldn't win, whichever pawns I used or where I placed them, but DI Locke's absorption in my father's offences was a useful tool to dispense of the shame I felt for lying to her.

Lewis pushed open the door. It was supposed to have been our last night in Wales. Two weeks had passed in a semi-conscious blur of visits to the CID unit in Cwmbran, questions over coffee, and whispered words in bed. Not to mention the research I'd pored over, often watching the sun set and rise before I eventually closed my eyes to sleep, drifting seamlessly from one nightmare to another until I woke up drenched in sweat, tears streaming down my face, and with Lewis' sleepy concerned eyes staring back at me as I pummelled at his chest, thrashing and kicking and screaming.

He never asked me what I was frightened of, or what it was that made me panic the moment he removed his clothes or closed the door of our small but comfortable B&B bedroom. He assumed it was travelling back to the town where the horrors of my father's crimes had been carried out. He did not suspect it had anything to do with its connection to my own childhood.

I had no intention of broaching the subject, because once I did, I'd have to explain Iefan's biology, and somewhere at the back of my mind I was scared their shared genetic code meant our eldest son had inherited my father's diseased mind.

Or perhaps *I* had.

Arriving back in Brynmawr had changed me. I was willing to cover for Gwenda's tenacity to murder.

I remembered the places I visited with my parents as a child for weekend daytrips or half-term holidays. My father might have had the opportunity to dispose of the girls bodies at any one of those sites when he took his sand-coated car to valet while me and my mother stood watching the sun lower on the horizon, listened to the splash of waves, felt the gentle caress of the evening breeze on the exposed parts of our skin in Porthcawl. Or the weekend treks through the meadows and valleys bordering our home from the river and dense woodland that left us tired and hungry.

Seren and Siân could be anywhere.

# BRYN

*Brynmawr, Ebbw Vale, Wales, 1994*

Seren's hopeful eyes pleaded with Bryn's. Her wrists and ankles were bound together, forcing her body into an *O* shape to ensure she wouldn't make too much noise thrashing around in her attempt to escape. She begged him to let her go but all that came out of her gagged mouth was a moan.

Her satin green dress dragged across the dirty basement floor as he tugged her by the hair, dropping her onto the mattress. She no longer looked like a terrified twelve-year-old girl, but a disobedient teenager who needed to be punished.

He left her, hair caked in grime, bloodied knees from where they'd scraped across the rough concrete, choking on her own tears, sobbing, shaking, and retching.

She lay on her side over the filthy mattress, her tights ripped, bare legs scuffed and bruised, facing the wall furthest from the stone-cold steps.

He locked the basement door and turned toward the hall where his wife, key angled in his direction stood motionless, eyes narrowed, face glinting with perspiration.

'Finally decided to tidy up have you?'

Relief forced his shoulders to drop an inch, the tension in his muscles dissipating. She was unaware there was a girl down there. 'You'd only nag me otherwise.'

'What brought all this on?' she waved a hand at the piles of rubbish he'd had to remove from the basement to make way for his love-nest down below.

'I've been preoccupied recently, but I've decided to clean up and get rid.'

She had no idea he was talking about the girl whose continued defiance had forced him to admit he could no longer hold her captive. She had to go. It wasn't wise to keep her tied up in the basement. Not if she kept banging and clattering around. Without the added insulation of boxes filled with clutter, the sounds would echo, and it was only a matter of time before Rhiannon or Carys heard the commotion and decided to investigate the cause of the noise they falsely believed to be rats.

His face hot and clammy from the exertion, arms aching from pulling her around, he'd chosen to dispose of Seren as soon as the opportunity arose.

He hadn't meant to hurt her. Had only, seeing her walking to her dance lesson alone, offered to drive her there to ensure her safe arrival. But then she'd smiled at him, fluttering her innocent lashes, and laughed at his jokes, and when he offered to drive her back to the farm, to lie to her parents for her so she wouldn't have to attend the lesson her mother had paid for but that she did not want to attend, she'd agreed.

He'd led her down into the basement to listen to pop music her mother didn't allow, being a Jehovah's witness like his wife.

Seren wanted to experience the same things her peers did, and he was only too willing to show her. He took his time, building her trust, complimenting her, turning her slowly against the mother who she felt had abandoned her for the cult-like worshippers she gave her fullest attention to. Just like Rhiannon.

'Why don't you stay here, teach your mother a lesson? She'll appreciate you more if you disappeared for a while.'

She looked unsure, but he reasoned it was fear that drove her eyes toward the door at regular intervals. He didn't have long to build a rapport with her. Rhiannon would be home soon, then he'd have to collect Carys from school.

'I can't have you making noises, it would upset my wife. And my daughter would be jealous if she knew you were here. If she found out I was giving all my attention to another little girl. She can be very sullen when she wants to be.'

Seren was complicit as he wrapped her pearl white cardigan around her mouth, hesitated a moment before submitting to the leather straps he used to bind her wrists and ankles together which he attached to the wooden ceiling beam. And when he returned that night, his anticipation and excitement was excruciating. He had to have her. Make her his.

She fought him as he knew she would, which served only to anger him. He hadn't thought the plan through as logically as intended.

He remembered his father teaching him to

harvest. 'Practice makes a wise man brave,' he said.

Seren was testing his patience. He knew he had to do better next time. Suppress his urges and get to know the girl before he broke her. He'd been fantasising for so long he'd almost forgotten the purpose. He wanted the perfect victim. One who did not require the need to be tied up and locked in. He wanted a girl who looked like Carys, but who wasn't as old or as petulant.

His next victim would be younger still. Perhaps nine or ten. Easier to tame.

He crept down to the basement the following morning, once his wife and daughter were safely out of the house, removing the cardigan from Seren's mouth as she lay limp on the edge of the mattress, looking up at him as he removed the straps from her rake-thin arms, leaving a jagged red pattern where the leather had bit into her flesh. He didn't want to hurt her, but he couldn't let her go home. Not now he had got what he wanted.

'Where are we going?' she stuttered through raspy tear-soaked lips, as he pulled her to her feet and escorted her hastily up the steps and across the hall toward the back door.

'To the woods.'

She didn't ask him why, just followed his footsteps to the kitchen and out into the sunshine. Feeling the balmy heat on her face. He watched and listened as she breathed in the fresh summer air and he wished it didn't have to end this way.

She was beautiful. She looked just like Carys had in her youth. Except unlike her, Seren would never grow older. She'd be dead before noon.

He moved her swiftly down the garden and into the paddock, glancing around in case anyone saw them together, recognised the missing girl, and rightly predicted he was responsible for her abduction, but there was not a soul nearby. He relaxed his posture and pulled her hurriedly along the paddock, past the stables, the barn, and down toward the pig sty.

*Pigs can crush and swallow human bones. If you starve them long enough, they'll eat anything*, his father's words resounded through his skull.

It was a good job he lived on a farm, he thought. He could reuse their faeces as manure, and nobody need ever know Seren Lloyd had been there at all.

# CARYS

*Brynmawr, Ebbw Vale, Wales, 2018*

'My apologies for asking you to come in at such short notice,' said DI Locke.

I watched her smooth down her crisp white shirt and wondered if it was a delaying tactic to unsettle me.

'I've asked you here today to speak to you some more about your mother, Rhiannon. She was a Jehovah's witness, is that correct?'

She knew she was. The Ebbw Vale Valley News Online had already used it as a basis to convict my mother of accessory to murder times three. The public declaring: 'how could his wife not know what he was up to?'

'Yes.'

'Your mother passed away in 1998, when you were

sixteen years old.'

'Uh, huh.'

'We've spoken to one of your late parent's friends, who came forward suggesting your mother's behaviour changed somewhat due to her illness.'

'She suffered migraines and vision disturbances. She often felt nauseous and dizzy. She tripped over a few times. Would get drowsy. She fell into a coma, slipped down the stairs, was admitted to hospital, and was diagnosed with diabetes.'

She glanced at her colleague and I started to get irritated by her deliberate stalling tactics. 'She was referred to a specialist diabetic nurse who offered her a treatment plan which included insulin, but she refused to take it.'

I nodded this time. I couldn't be bothered to reply.

'The nurse, Gwendalyn Kavanagh was a follower of the Jehovah's Witness movement in Abergavenny.' She was noting my reaction.

'Gwenda-lyn? She knew my mother?'

It was DI Locke's turn to nod.

'Aside from in a professional capacity at the hospital, it looks like they spent at least one evening each week seated near each other during the Friday fellowship meeting held in the Kingdom Hall.'

That was my chance to tell her I suspected Gwenda had got close to my father with the sole intention of murdering him. But I could have been in danger from Gwenda if she'd discovered I'd snitched on her.

'It's possible your mother met Siân.

She left the accusing comment at that, hoping I'd fill in the missing words from the sentence, but I offered her a blank stare. I wasn't ready to admit my mother's talk of rats beneath the house might have been a cover for the sounds I heard regularly coming through the floor. One time it sounded like something heavy was being dragged across the concrete under my bedroom, but not knowing the basement was there I determined it must have been my father moving things around in the ever-cluttered hallway in front of the broom cupboard where my father had raised the carpet to expose and dry out the damp floorboards. My mother dismissed my concerns about vermin climbing inside the walls, but she was clenching and unclenching her hands in anxiety and her eyes gave away something close to fear, so I dropped the subject.

Why had I not questioned her further?

*You were a child, Carys. You couldn't have known what awful things your father had been doing.*

But was my mother aware of the monster she had married? And if so, why had she allowed it to continue right under her nose?

'How did you and your father feel about your mother's beliefs?'

'My father disliked her religion. He said it was a cult. She never attempted to conform me to the principles she lived by, but she did try to pressure my father into attending meetings with her. He refused.'

'Your mother had some problems with certain members of the community I believe.'

'She regularly protested for the abolition of medical termination. Her and her cronies used to stand outside the sexual health clinic with pro-life petitioners or distributing leaflets outside doctor's surgeries containing pictures of aborted foetuses. She claimed they continued to live after being removed, could still breathe, were capable of feeling pain.'

'Your mothers friend suggested she wouldn't have been pleased about the legalization of same sex marriage.'

'She banned me from continuing to work in the bookshop a few weeks before she died when she discovered the owner was gay. She slammed the door on his partners face when he dropped by to hand over my final lot of wages the day before her death. She viewed same sex relationships as a sin.'

'How do you think she would have reacted to the news that Ella, who was underage, was pregnant?'

'Nobody knew who Ella was until you identified her bones. Her disappearance wasn't news here.'

Then it clicked. DI Locke thought my mother abducted Ella to prevent her from having a termination.

'You think Rhiannon kept her locked up in the basement to assist with the birth?'

*And covered up her death to prevent anyone from finding out that the child Ella was carrying was your fathers?*

'We have got to cover every option, Carys. I'm sure you understand.'

'I do,' I said, whipping my handbag up from the table and hanging it over my shoulder. 'You think my mother knew Ella's baby was my fathers, that she was complicit in her husband's, my father's, crimes?'

'I'd like to know more about your relationship with Rhiannon. If I can eliminate your mother's potential involvement in the girl's abuse, I can rule out several leads that could postpone my directive.'

'You're not interested in the truth, you just need someone to condemn, no matter how that reflects on me or affects my family. Have you any idea what we're going through?'

I didn't give her time to reply.

'We were supposed to have come here to tidy up the farm, put it on the market, and hope the sale would be quick enough for us to use the money to buy somewhere bigger to live in Bristol before the house prices sky-rocket again. But now the police and press are trampling all over the farm, I'm being followed and glared at every time I return to this god-forsaken town by journalists, and the local gossipers don't give a shit how it's impacting on my boys. I couldn't care less who was involved in my father's sick, perverted crimes. It's hideous, but I just want you to find Seren and Siân and put this whole sorry saga to rest.'

I could feel my nerves teetering on the edge of rage. I forced myself to breathe normally and silently thanked DI Locke for remaining untouched by my outburst.

'I understand how hard this is for you. It's difficult to hear things about those close to us that perhaps we were unaware of or struggle to accept are true. But, before you go, I have one more question.'

I turned, resting my hand on the doorknob, about to depart.

'Your mother's occupation before you were born, what was it?'

'She was a phlebotomist.'

'Where did she work?'

'The Royal Gwent hospital.'

'Thank you, Carys. You've been very helpful.'

'What's my mother's previous employment got to do with . . . hold on, isn't that where Gwenda worked?'

'I'm sorry. I can't divulge confidential information, especially when it pertains to a case. But there's nothing stopping you from asking her, is there?'

I left the police station to meet the hot throbbing sun, feeling my face burn from a mixture of the late morning heat and the embarrassment of discovering – not from my own investigative work, but from the detective – that Gwenda probably worked with my mother at the hospital where they both would have had access to patient notes including those which contained the details of pregnant young women.

The term baby farming came to mind, though without finding any more remains how could I or the police prove that was how my mother selected the girls my father could abuse and impregnate?

It wasn't until I reached the car that I thought about the family friend insinuated by DI Locke to have implicated my mother for the girl's abductions. It had to have been Bill Erwin. But what would motivate such a loyally devoted follower of Jehovah to incriminate Rhiannon?

# GWENDA

*Brynmawr, Ebbw Vale, Wales, 1995*

Gwendalyn dropped her full name the moment she was old enough to write. She took pride in her appearance, never feeling quite as though she fitted in with her peers. She always felt slightly shut off from the world as if the society she lived within didn't understand her. Or maybe she'd been born into the wrong era, the wrong family. Whatever the reason, she didn't quite get *them*. Perhaps that too was the reason for her eccentricity in style.

Her house was decorated in an array of bright bold colours. And the clothes she wore weren't much different. It didn't stop her finding a kind handsome gentleman to date during one long, lonely summer though.

Siân was born the following spring.

Siân was a hippy child with Gaelic roots. Gwenda found her daughters temperament one of a mixture between an earthy roamer and a spoilt brat. But she adored her quirkiness, and when she developed her own sense of fashionwear, she knew who she'd inherited it from.

A week before she'd gone missing, they'd just arrived home from a trip to the nearby ruins of a castle set deep in the valleys overlooking the violet forget-me-not landscape. It was there that Gwenda feared she'd set the precedent for things to come.

Siân was a wilful child, curious, and spontaneous. Outgoing they'd call her now, insolent her teachers called her then. She was unafraid to tell you how she felt, and it meant Gwenda didn't much worry about her getting into mischief, knowing she'd find a way to tear herself out of it when it occurred.

The day Siân disappeared Gwenda had a new washing machine delivery. She was sat on the front step of the porch reading the newspaper and waiting for it to arrive. Siân was playing hopscotch on the pavement at the end of the road where one of the neighbouring children had drawn the numbered squares with chalk. Old Mrs Hodges was hanging her whites up on the line in front of her house. It had begun to rain when Kian had run through the gate to alert her of the blue car that he'd seen Siân jump into. She dropped the newspaper and fled to the bottom of the road, but it was too late, Siân was gone.

Over the coming months she garnered leads from the police and information from gossips in the corner shop, eventually coming to the conclusion that the man who'd taken her daughter lived out of town, owned a blue vehicle of some type- although nobody could verify Kian's description and the detectives weren't interested in looking into every Ford driven within one hundred miles of the area at the time of the incident for fear that trusting a child's testimony could waste valuable resources and everyone's time. The local search parties soon died down and eventually Gwenda resigned to never seeing her daughter again.

But she never stopped believing Siân was out there somewhere, alive, and spent every conceivable moment she could looking for her, hoping it was to no avail.

Siân's father blamed himself. Working out of town when his daughter had been taken. He sank into a deep depression that he never came out of. Amd eventually the pressure this put on their relationship forced them apart.

When she saw the smoke billowing out of the garage door, heard the engine of his navy-blue car running, and smelt the heavy exhaust fumes, she raised the door and found him hanging by a tow rope attached to a hook he'd mounted to the ceiling.

# CARYS

*Brynmawr, Ebbw Vale, Wales, 1995*

Wind whistled through the eaves of the house as I made my way toward the paddock. The gale brewed to a crescendo. It roared as I edged further away from the farm. A slow torturous breath catching the funnel of the chimney. My father had warned me not to tread as far as the paddock, but I was a bored twelve-year-old with no siblings to play with.

I'd passed the pigs on my way to the woods, felt a tingling sensation coat my skin as though someone was watching me, hoping it wasn't my father. I held a hand over my forehead to block the sun from my eyes but saw only the empty windows of the farmhouse, my mother having removed the curtains to wash. I continued to amble along the uneven terrain, a darkness sweeping over me as I passed a mound of freshly dug earth near the dense woodland, the feeling of negativity intensifying as I neared the sty.

I had no qualms about leaving the place I'd grown up in as soon as I were able. But I would have to stay as far away from my father as possible until I was old enough to gather my possessions and run. I did not know where I would go or what future lay in front of me. Escape was my only aim. So I spent most of my time after school outside, watching the changing seasons turn the landscape from green to yellow, to red, to brown, to white, and back again.

I caught up with my father at the clearing leading into the dense forest. He was seemingly unaware of my presence, standing out in the sun with his back to me, staring off into the distance. His once thick hair had thinned and turned blond from the sun and his skin glowed brown.

I knew one day he'd do something awful. I wanted to tell my mother, who seemed unaware, about the bedtime stories that made me uncomfortable. I wanted to warn her he looked at young girls in the same way that he looked at her when he thought I wouldn't notice. I wanted her to discover Bryn leering at me through the gap in the bathroom door he said was supposed to remain partway open to ensure I didn't get locked in if the handle fell off or jammed like it had once before. But I couldn't tell my mother, didn't know what words to use, felt afraid of her reaction, so I kept quiet and tried to avoid him as much as possible. But in bed I couldn't abscond. He looked, rubbed, sighed, and gasped, and all the while I closed my eyes and pretended that I could fly out of my bedroom window and over the valleys and meadowland to seek refuge in the forestry so that the goblin king and his fairy companions could welcome me in, and take me to safety.

'Come take a walk with me,' my father often said.

Sometimes I got out of hiking by helping my mother dish up the meal she'd been 'slaving over' all afternoon, cleaning out the chicken coop, or mucking out the horses until my father retreated to his desk in the study beside my bedroom overlooking the golden landscape.

When he was preoccupied, I was safe.

He showed me a bird's nest once. He saved the winged family after discovering their home had toppled onto the ground beneath the large leafy Sycamore tree in a storm. He'd re-attached the nest to a branch with some wire to hold it in place. The mother had come in the night to bring her children some worms to eat. 'Now they're safe from predators, fed, warm, and dry.'

Bryn could be kind when he wanted to be.

We used to go shopping together, or visit the library when mum wasn't well. He held my hand and lifted me over stiles that were too high for my short legs to climb. Sometimes we played hide and seek or tag. Those days existed, but they always ended the same.

I slept fitfully until woken up by the creaking of the door. It was almost dawn and my mother snored loudly from down the hall while my father sidled against me, pressing himself into my spine, breathing heavily onto my neck. I wanted to scream, to cry, or shove him away, but felt paralysed, numb.

Always in the back of my mind I knew I would be free of my father one day, in the distant future, and that thought was what I lived in hope for though it wasn't enough to quell the overwhelming panic of the present.

He acted distant in public, but in the confines of our home his deferent behaviour evoked a kind of fear within me that was difficult to articulate least of all understand and left me wondering if he realised he was splitting, decompartmentalizing the two sides to his personality. And if others noticed it too.

That was when I began writing my thoughts down, to try to make sense of them. My diary became a lifeline. Until I lost it. I feared my mother had found it, but if she had wouldn't she have said something?

# GWENDA

*Brynmawr, Ebbw Vale, Wales, 2015*

Gwenda air-kissed her colleagues goodbye, tearful and excited at the same time for leaving her post and venturing into retirement. She left the hospital for the final time as an employee, having served thirty-five years in various departments under the banner of a General Nursing Practitioner with an awkward smile on her face.

She took the lift down to the ground floor carrying two bouquets of plum and bright yellow carnations, a huge card signed by the staff and some of the long-term stay patients from the diabetic ward. She fingered the photograph of her late born, one and only, missing daughter as she slowed her footing in the corridor to glance around the building one last time.

She'd miss the place. The sounds, the smells. Some nice, some not so nice. The staff, the patients. The warmth of the ward she'd spent so many months working on.

She thought back to her various positions over the past three and a half decades, remembering the day she'd been sent to treat Rhiannon.

It was her eyes that gave her guilt away. She knew something, and the more Gwenda pressed, the closer she got to learning who the mysterious man Rhiannon, always seated one row behind her during a meeting at the Kingdom Hall was married to. And soon, she would come face to face with Bryn Howell, her daughter's murderer, who it turned out Kian had correctly identified as the driver of the blue car that he was adamant Siân had been lured into.

Once the grief had worn thin, overshadowed by an innate need to investigate the claims herself, Gwenda had scoured countless leads, talking to anyone who'd listen, making friends wherever she went, hoping that one day someone somewhere would provide her with enough information to further her case. But it turned out the person responsible had been closer than she thought.

It was two years after Siân's disappearance when Rhiannon entered the lobby of the meeting room housed inside an old warehouse, bought and done up by the elder, that Gwenda temporarily left the fog of grief behind long enough to realise how distant Rhiannon had become since they had first spoken. And it was she who suggested they leave the meeting together.

It was sipping coffee across a mahogany table in the café that a group of them used to visit often that her world was shattered.

Gwenda instigated the conversation, detailing the horrific expense of owning a car, declaring herself to be a lover of classics, hoping to lull Rhiannon into a false sense of trust as she did with everyone she met and spoke to, hoping one day a lifeline would be thrown at her. Her plan paid off. Rhiannon slipped up.

'My husband owned an old blue whatsit. You know the ones with the central locking defect.'

The only ones with that problem were pale blue. She sat up straighter, listening intently, feigning a blasé attitude to the discussion while her heart hammered in her chest. Kian said the man who'd taken Siân had thick hair, receding slightly up top. He had a large muscular frame and a weathered look about him, as if he worked outdoors all day. Gwenda had almost dismissed Bryn as the culprit because he was an accountant – didn't they wear suits and ties? – but Rhiannon lived on a farm. Bryn worked from home. He could wear whatever he liked.

'We've got hens, sheep, horses, and pigs,' said Rhiannon.

Gwenda clenched her jaw tight and tried to smile, fearing something she'd heard from a film might be possible: that pigs ate human bones when starved.

Gwenda took some time away from the fellowship, deciding how to approach Bryn Howell over his sins. But when Bill Erwin, noticing she'd started to lose faith since her daughter had gone missing informed her that Rhiannon had been admitted to the diabetic ward, she suggested visiting her. That was her gateway.

Rhiannon was surprised to see Gwenda arrive at the hospital, wearing her uniform after leaving a shift in Gloucester Royal.

'I didn't know you worked here?'

She didn't but the uniform in Gwent Royal was the same colour as it was throughout the country.

Without the lanyard containing her ID card – the only thing that would have given away the name of the trust she worked for – around her neck Rhiannon made it so easy for her to lie. Even Gwenda was a little surprised to find how easy it came to her.

Gwenda pushed Rhiannon to talk about her daughter, steering the subject back to her own. She knew from the way Rhiannon responded to the mere mention of the ongoing investigation, becoming either dismissive or attempting to avoid the topic altogether, that although she might not have known what her husband was up to, she wore guilt like a badge of honour.

Was she an enabler?

She had no need to alter Rhiannon's Observation and Continuous Monitoring scales, which was her first idea. Her prognosis wasn't good. If she didn't take insulin, she'd be dead in a couple of years. She had her Witness version of the King James Bible to hand and quoted several references to trusting Jehovah, surrendering to his will, and assured her that pharmaceutical intervention was used by the government to control the public by putting them on medications they had no need for. 'God provides for those who repent.'

Within less than an hour she was able to convince Rhiannon to discharge herself from hospital and, to please her husband and doctor, continue collecting her pills but take them infrequently. Which she did until her health gradually worsened, and she died.

She thought Rhiannon's passing would come sooner than it did. She thought it would satisfy her need for justice. She continued working in the hospital, but gradually, over the years, and especially after her retirement, with Bryn Howell having been seemingly unaffected by his wife's demise according to the members of her prayer group she remained in contact with for the sole purpose of gathering information about his life, she grew bitter and angry.

From her home in Abergavenny she conducted a fool-proof plan to befriend Bryn, but to get it right required planning, timing, cunning, and surveillance. She narrowed it down to one weekend in autumn, when lonely, cold, isolated, and likely in pain according to the computed medical notes she'd read when accessing his patient records through her temporary log-in before her boss closed the account down within days of her retirement, Gwenda bumped into him after waiting in the lane for three hours. Her feet were numb from the cold and her jacket was drenched from the rain. She befriended Bryn Howell, intending to fleece him of everything he owned.

What, she thought, would hurt a financial expert more than physical pain? Losing all his beloved possessions. His money. His house. And then, his life.

The day he invited Gwenda into the farm, crossing the threshold before her, licking his lips in anticipation as he showed her to a seat where she was able to view the photograph of Carys – her rose blonde wavy hair and bright blue eyes reminding her of her own daughter – she felt she'd found what she'd been searching for, for years. The truth.

'Tea, coffee? I have whiskey too if you'd like a drop of something less lady-like?'

'Coffee will be fine. Thank you,' she said, giving him a tight smile while she gazed into his shallow filthy-minded eyes and vowed to avenge her daughters murder.

It didn't matter how long it took to convince Bryn she was a woman he could count on and was worth leaving his worldly possessions to, she'd do it.

As soon as his back was turned, and he'd left the

room she closer inspected the photograph of his only daughter, the one who'd fled her childhood home aged sixteen, suddenly it appeared. Though according to Bill she'd left having fallen pregnant underage, defiling her family name.

Carys' features wore the same haunted expression she'd witnessed on a young girl who'd been admitted to her care during her nursing training. She'd arrived with a fractured wrist and bruised torso. When her father walked into the room the girl had lowered her head and could barely look Gwenda in the eyes as she answered her questions in a low childlike voice, despite her seventeen years.

The knife-edge atmosphere and the abject shame in the girl's face told her the girl's father had hurt her. It was the same maternal tug she felt when gazing into Carys' sad eyes. Aged six the pencilled handwriting said when she tore the back off the gilded frame. She set it back into the position she'd found it in just before Bryn re-entered the room carrying two china cups on beautifully decorated saucers.

Without doubt Bryn had abused that girl. It was evident in her eyes. A deep penetrating sadness, unnoticeable to those who didn't know what they were looking for. But which she, with all her years of medical experience and the brief safeguarding training she'd been instructed to attend, gave her the knowledge she needed to presume the reason Carys had run from her childhood home at the age of legal consent was to escape her predatory father. Perhaps the child Carys had been carrying was his. But she couldn't make such strong allegations without confirmation.

# CARYS

*Brynmawr, Ebbw Vale, Wales, 1995*

Bill Erwin opened the door of his house and stepped aside, allowing me to enter. I felt his eyes caress my skin from behind, and shivered as he led me down the hall, past the kitchen and into the conservatory he'd recently had built.

Bill liked to show off his wealth. And that day as I sat beside him on a floral cushioned wicker chair overlooking the vast expanse of inch-short lawn he paid a local gardener to mow each week, he told me all about his recent sale of a navy-blue car to Joe Sykes. 'An Irishman. Lives with some woman up in Abergavenny. She's one of us.'

Bill often tried to win me over to the beliefs he shared with my mother. It seemed everybody was turning their backs on celebrating Christmas and

New Year for the Jehovah's Witness movement. Even Joe Sykes, who's 'live-in partner' Bill said with contempt, sat in the same row as him every Friday in the Kingdom Hall without Joe seated in support beside her.

'I've been trying to persuade your father to attend a meeting for years but he's a hard one to crack too,' he laughed.

He moved closer to hand me a beaker of diluted orange squash to sip with the packet of Custard Creams I was eating. 'You're not.'

'Not what?' I looked up at him with wide curious eyes.

'Difficult to read,' he said. 'Good at keeping secrets so your father says. But I can see, if you don't mind my saying so, you'd rather talk about them.'

'Talk about what?'

'Whatever turns your face to stone whenever I mention your father's name.' He lowered his voice and added, 'some secrets aren't meant to be kept.'

I was beginning to get uncomfortable from the *thing* he was insinuating.

'I'm not an ogre, Carys.' He smiled weakly. 'It's scary being a kid. I was one once.' He laughed at his own joke. I cringed inwardly. 'It's good to have someone to confide in. You've got friends in school you can talk to if something's bothering you, haven't you?'

I shook my head.

'Well, I'm here. If ever you need to get something off your chest.'

I nodded quickly, while he sat up straighter. Then it was *he* who was starting to look uncomfortable.

I wondered if he knew what my father did to me. If, during one of his visits to the farm Bill had discovered my diary and taken it home to read, and perhaps that was why I couldn't find it.

When he went to answer the phone down the hall, I scoured the living room quickly, then excused myself to the bathroom, getting a nod of acknowledgement from Bill before he turned his back on me, whispering down the receiver. I began hunting the upstairs stealthily while he chatted to Joe Sykes, who appeared to be his latest target. From Bill's one-sided conversation, I could tell they were on friendly terms. But when he put the phone down – I'd already returned to the living room without finding my diary anywhere in the house – he said, 'not interested. Lost cause that man. Doesn't want to hear The Truth.'

I nodded slowly, pretending to understand why Bill and my mother went out of their way, wasting their time, to lure people toward their skewed faith if no one was really interested in listening to their version of the bible.

Bill glanced down at his watch. 'Time you got home, eh? Your parents will be wondering where you are.'

I shook my head. 'Father didn't show up to collect me from school, and mother got the bus to the new medical practice that's opened in Abergavenny.'

'Bryn's a busy man, but I'd have expected him to take fifteen minutes out of his day to pick you up from school,' he said, trying to sound the words jokingly although I knew he really meant them. My father had done it several times before. Then he smiled. 'At least your mum has got her priorities right. Fellowship is on par with prayer.'

I didn't think holding banners and shouting at people was a godly thing to do, but then neither was speaking ill of those who weren't there to defend themselves, so I clamped my mouth shut.

I was barely listening when he said who my

mother had attended the protest that they called *Fellowship* with.

'Lynne or Lyndsey or something like that. Irishwoman. She travels down from Abergavenny each week. Hasn't missed a meeting in months.'

# RHIANNON

*Abergavenny, Wales, 1995*

Rhiannon clenched her placard baring the poster she'd drawn and taped onto it. Her knuckles turned white as she gripped the pole harder at the sight of the young mothers who ignored her and Gwendalyn as they raised their voices to the wind to deliver their rehearsed speech.

'The Lord damns those to hell who forsake his teaching. May you be replenished of your sins and bathed in his divine glory.'

When that didn't draw a reaction from the gathering crowd of local mothers who had stormed toward them demanding to know why they displayed enlarged pictures of aborted foetuses directly opposite a primary school, their voices grew louder.

'Killing the innocent for your own selfish sexual

perversions is an abomination. The man who gave you life condemns you sinners!'

They were cursed and spat at, but it only served to make them more determined to change the minds of the female patients entering the medical practice.

A man, tall and beefy, came up close and pointing at Rhiannon and Gwendalyn laughed. 'This is a doctor's surgery you stupid cows. No one's coming in here getting a termination.'

'This is where the initial appointment is made,' said Rhiannon.

He shook his head, tutted, turned, and walked away.

After an hour of standing out in the heat, Gwendalyn nudged her, 'I've got to leave before 11:00am. I've got my new washing machine being delivered then I have a ton of ironing to do. I won't be able to relax until I bring Siân home from school.'

'Couldn't Joe pick her up?'

'No. He's working in Ebbw Vale today. Thanks to Bill, he's been able to accept a few jobs out of town,' said Gwendalyn.

'I'll have to have a word with Bill on Friday. My husband's been looking for a new car for ages.'

*

Returning to the farm around lunchtime, Rhiannon hurriedly undressed, changed into her house clothes, made herself a ham and tomato sandwich, and ate it quickly, planning to walk the three miles into town, having used up all her allowance on the bus fare to Abergavenny that morning.

She was going to visit the Christian book shop in town to ask the manager if he'd give Carys a job the following summer. With few workplace choices nearby parents had been urged to organise their children's work-experience ahead of time. A year before was probably considered too early, but the manager was leaving in a few weeks, and she wanted to get Carys' name put on the list before the new boss arrived. She hoped it would be a man. Carys listened to her father far better than she did to her.

It was as she was stuffing her feet inside her brown suede boots, purchased impulsively from a charity shop for their comfort; the heels at a suitable level for a woman of her pedigree, that she found the diary stuffed against the wall as though Carys had hidden it behind the shoe rack in the hallway in her haste to deposit it. Perhaps she'd been late for school and had brought it to the door with her by mistake.

She bent to retrieve it, intending to leave it upstairs on Carys' bed, so she'd find it the moment she entered her room.

It was almost 2:00pm by the time Rhiannon made it to the library. Leaving the building late, she called Bryn at home to ask him to escape his study to collect Carys from school, but the phone just rang and rang.

# PART TWO

# CARYS

*Redland, Bristol, England, 2018*

Returning home to Bristol had been Lewis' idea. Though I still felt something magnetizing me to stay in Brynmawr, I had no reason to refuse to come home. The studio needed me behind the camera, but I was reluctant to leave Wales before we'd listed the renovations needed to put the property on the market. I couldn't begin calling companies least of all employ anyone based on a quote via a phone call. I wanted to ask around, meet people, view portfolio's, and maybe visit one or two houses the roofers, carpenters, plumbers, electricians, and plasterers had recently completed work on to review their work and gain some testimonials. I couldn't do that from a distance.

The police were continuing to dig up the farm, the

mess accumulating and stalling my plans. They seemingly had no intention of returning the garden, paddock, or two-acre field beyond to a decent state any time soon according to DI Locke. A landscaper was not going to commit to such a large spacious area alone, so the financial investment required to employ several groundsmen was going to be substantially more than expected.

I'd spoken to Gwenda intermittently through the rising and dipping signal on our journey back to Bristol that morning, apologising for not being able to say goodbye before we left, not wanting to see the farm in such a state of half-completed excavation as we passed it to reach her house. In her words the farm was a 'sorry mess' and she herself was considering selling up. 'I can see the house from my garden. Knowing what happened there . . . I can't bear it.'

I was also avoiding her. I wasn't sure I could trust Gwenda after I'd learned she'd lied to me, had given the police a different version of events surrounding the discovery of my dead father. I also wondered what it meant knowing she had befriended Bryn after her daughter had disappeared whom the police had just discovered he may have abducted. That she had at one time worked in the same hospital as my mother and had sat a row behind Rhiannon in the Kingdom Hall each week.

If she'd killed my father, it was possible she'd killed my mother too. She'd worked on both diabetic and cardiology wards during her nursing career.

Rubble, and rubbish was a concern I could live with. Having your daughter stolen, sexually brutalised, and murdered was something I thankfully had never experienced. So the renovations on the farm could wait.

I watched on the television screen, Ella James' mother sob with a tissue pressed to her nose and her head rested against her husband's. Not Ella's father. He'd died two years previously. The poor woman was in the process of arranging a funeral, the coroner having finally released her daughters remains for burial. It seemed Ella had spent a birthday and Christmas on the property as the DNA sample taken from her toothbrush and hairbrush after she'd gone missing, matched blood on a magazine dated ten months after her disappearance that was found inside a box in the basement in the house my father owned, along with a water bottle she'd drunk from. Luminol spray showed blood splatter on the mattress I'd assumed was covered in dirt that I'd seen in the basement the day we'd visited the farm to start shifting stuff.

My intuition had been telling me something was wrong with the damp cluttered space, and I vowed never to ignore it again. I was glad I had listened to it that day, because if I hadn't, I may not have continued rooting through the farm and found Ella's daughter- my sister. I might have focussed wrongly on the unease of the basement rather than investigate the outbuildings which led me to discover the infants remains in the water-logged paddock. And the police would not have uncovered Ella's skeleton nor my father's insidious crimes.

I tried not to, but I couldn't stop myself from imagining what my baby sister might have looked like if she'd have survived. Would she have inherited my eye colour, bone structure, love of art?

I stared at the television screen even after Lewis had switched it off. I felt a blanket being draped over me, a hot cup of sugary tea pressed against my lips, his fingers smoothing down my hair. 'Isn't it a bit soon to return to the studio?'

Work was all I had available to switch my mind off the awfulness of our situation. 'I'm going in.'

I had Sharon doing the prints in the dark room, arranging orders, and dealing with the printers for the canvases. She'd been holding the fort for three weeks. I was going to offer her a seven day all expenses paid holiday to thank her for her generous last-minute offer to manage the place after the news of my father's death, the fortnights planned visit to Ebbw Vale, and the unexpected need to stay longer than anticipated when I'd found the bones.

The studio was my sanctuary. Nothing would keep me from it. The repetitive actions of snapping photographs, downloading them onto the computer, dissecting their suitability to print in negative format, dividing the good from the great, re-arranging them, polishing them up, altering their size. Then the process of printmaking. Enlargement, silver plating, fixing the safelight on the exposure, dodging, burning, preparing the chemicals, immersion in developer, stopping, fixing, and washing in water trays before hanging each print up to dry. A time-consuming process, often easier to maintain patience for if I'd planned on outsourcing canvass versions. Which I did not prepare myself in-house and that meant I only had to digitise then buff them. But I preferred to do all the work myself. Keeping busy kept my mind off things.

The best part for me was travelling with a CD in the car belting out one of my favourite tunes, allowing my brainwaves to rest, before stopping someplace to snap pictures of historical buildings, wildlife, or willing volunteers.

Photography was a lengthy process, but the aim was to steal moments of the present that could be recorded for the future, that once printed would become subjectively considered scenes from the past. I studied art history, but found my passion not in oil painting, pottery, cross-stitching, card-making, or pencil drawing, but in snatching memories from the things I'd seen as they were at the time.

I envied Gwenda's ability to forget, but also worried for her. If her memories were all she had as she aged then how would she cope if those relating to her daughter slipped away completely, never again to be remembered?

I took off to capture some shots of the church spire

that dazzled in the sunlight piercing through a bunch of cotton-like clouds at the bottom of the hill in the centre of Redland.

A bird flew overhead at the right moment and I began to click away. But when I flicked through the images I'd taken, moments later, the focus wasn't right on any of them. I tried to correct it for the next lot, but no matter the angle or distance the lens kept blurring each time. I gave up the moment the sun disappeared behind a thick slate grey cloud, cursing.

I needed a new focus.

It was later, back at home after leaving the sanctuary of the studio, the boys upstairs playing on their consoles, eating the snacks they'd stolen from the kitchen to replenish themselves midway through their gaming when, noticing how tired and despondent I'd become, Lewis suggested I begin a new project. 'You've been moping around the house since you returned home from work.'

During our trip to Brynmawr I'd managed to snap a few photographs of the valleys an hour before entering the farm and discovering Ella's new-born daughters remains. The beautiful landscape was set against the wind-torn backdrop of fallen trees cast beneath a dark foreboding skyline. I'd captured the contrast between the dense earth and uncontrollable weather perfectly.

'Why don't you use them somehow?' he said, pointing at the photographs I'd strewn all over the dining table to inspect while I tried to come up with a reason to destroy them. 'You could depict the investigation from the beginning: the girl's disappearances, followed by their murders, and hopefully, eventually the day they're laid to rest. Categorize their lives and deaths in chronological order, maybe include the areas where witnesses described last seeing them alive, followed by CSI dissecting the land for their remains, and up to the day they were buried.'

I glanced up at him, a weak smile spreading across my face. 'It's just a thought,' he said.

'I think it's a great idea.'

I could capture the grief and sorrow my father's actions had caused, and the injustice of his death. Create something positive from it all. I could use the money from the sale of my work to donate to The Missing and Exploited Children's Charity, the sponsored ads of which regularly appeared on my

Facebook newsfeed.

'You'll have to go back though, to Ebbw Vale.'

'Yes, but not right away. I can start to assemble the images I already have.'

Humans are prone to misinterpretation. But I didn't want to leave room for inaccurate representation. I had to begin the display with a historical reference to family, trust, innocence, youth, memory, and how those combined components could be destroyed by one single factor or character. Like my father.

# BRYN

*Brynmawr, Ebbw Vale, Wales, 2015*

Bryn lay prone on his bed staring at the ceiling, trying not to allow the pain in his joints to get the better of him. The thought of having to walk the three miles to the grocery shop to buy eggs, milk, and bread, the items he would have had to hand if his wife were still alive or the farm was still running as one, was almost too unbearable to think about.

He hoisted himself off the bed, dressed, and headed out into the rain unable to eat first as there were no bags of oats left in the kitchen cupboards. By the time he reached the gate his jacket was already soaked through and his feet squelched inside the cheap boots he'd worn thin. At the turning of the lane he saw a flash of red hair, heard a small dog panting, and came face to face with a rather odd-looking woman cowering beneath the overhanging bush, Wellingtons submerged in the scrubby wet earth at the lanes edge. He supposed she was the new owner of the cottage down the hill.

'Gwenda,' she said through chattering teeth, holding out her wet, shivering hand to introduce herself.

He shook it stiffly, said, 'Bryn Howell.' Then turned toward the road.

She asked him where he was headed in such awful weather. 'I need milk and bread,' he said curtly.

'I'm off to the local shop, down the way. To save you the bother I could grab your groceries for you. That way you can get back into the warm?'

He wasn't sure. The postman was the only person who passed the gate to his property. He hadn't invited anyone aside from Bill into his home since his wife had died seventeen years before. But it was cold, wet, and he felt miserable, so he conceded it was a good idea.

'That's a very kind offer, and I wouldn't normally accept but . . .' he looked up at the thick droplets of rain pelting down from the dismal sky and said, 'I'd be very grateful.'

She took his meagre list which he'd added a bottle of whiskey and a pound of ham to, considering he didn't need to carry it home himself, and watched her set off with her yappy terrier at her heel.

She was gone a while. But he wasn't concerned for her. Gwenda appeared more than capable of looking after herself. Confident. Distant. But then so was he. Perhaps they'd get on.

He was in the kitchen when he heard her knock. He'd just boiled the kettle, so to show his appreciation he thanked her for doing his shopping for him with the offer of a shared pot of tea and some Welsh Cakes. She nodded her approval and glanced around the room at his cluttered abode while she nibbled on the Welshie's – as he called them – like a mouse.

He nodded politely as she wittered on about retirement, loneliness, and her opinion on the importance of friendship as she aged.

He didn't know what possessed him to do it. He never would have invited anyone into his home until that day, but he had. Perhaps his routine needed shaking up a bit. He asked her what she did for a living, and at the knowledge of her prior career in nursing confided he struggled sometimes to walk into town, no longer able to drive nor afford a car on his measly private pension. The livestock that had once provided him with an income were long dead and buried in various locations in the paddock.

He should have thought of that when he'd buried the girls. He could have avoided arousing suspicion by planting the diseased carcasses of animals that had died along with them. But thankfully nobody had questioned his whereabouts or witnessed him with them, so no one could prove he'd been involved in their murders. And, compared to most sprees he'd read about there weren't many. He lost interest in jail-bate after the third girl. He had to get rid of her because, like the others, he couldn't trust her to keep her mouth shut.

Gwenda didn't hesitate to voice her thoughts as he followed her eyes around the room. 'The place could do with a bit of a tidy up too, if you don't mind me saying so. Perhaps I could come in once or twice a week and spruce the place up a bit?'

'I'd like that very much. The company would be nice too, Gwenda.'

'How about Wednesday, that's assuming you don't

have any plans?'

'Sounds good to me.'

'I'll see you then.'

'I'll look forward to it.'

He saw her out then crossed the hall and opened the back door. He stood a while staring at the ground in front of the barn where he'd buried his daughter. He turned slightly toward the side where Ella's remains were. His sight didn't reach as far back as the field beyond, but an ice-cold shiver ran down his spine as he caught the familiar treeline where the pig sty used to be as though drawn to where he'd buried the other girl.

Images of her danced in front of him.

Rose blonde hair.

Blue eyes.

Dainty features.

A beautiful emerald green dress that fit her perfectly and flowed out from her waist as she danced and spun and ran and fell.

The final words Seren had spoken haunted his dreams. She refused to cease taunting him even when he was awake. Sometimes he was sure he saw her, a shadow here, a blurred colour in his peripheral vision there. Watching, waiting for him to receive his comeuppance.

He knew his day would come, but he hoped that with Gwenda around he could live out the rest of his years in dignity before it occurred. Because, since he had ample time to think on it, if what Rhiannon believed about that religion of hers was true, he was going to hell.

# CARYS

*Redland, Bristol, England, 2018*

Lewis eyed me from across the waiting room, meeting me where I'd parked nearest the door, chest pounding, eyes trained to where the doctor would appear in a few moments.

The room was shaded in an array of pastel colours, ice pink, lemon, lime green, and baby blue. I flinched from the intrusive word: baby. But no matter how hard I tried I could not escape them, there in that Bristol surgery they were everywhere.

I hadn't told Lewis my truth. But I had admitted I was struggling to cope with all I had learned about my father. Although not once during our discussions about his deeds had I insinuated being a victim myself, I saw a hidden knowledge beneath Lewis' steady gaze I fought hard not to prove on some level he already knew and was waiting for me to disclose.

Since beginning the photography project I'd been able to manage my moods better, but the sinking feeling of desperation and helplessness I'd felt as a child had returned, and I didn't know what it meant, or how I could self-treat it. I needed a professional's opinion.

The bleep from the wall above me forced my eyes toward the screen to see my name lit up.

Lewis reached out to touch my hand as I departed, glancing down at the carpet when I didn't look at him.

Room four on the second floor was inhabited by a locum. I wasn't sure when I booked the appointment if it would make a difference, but having a female GP eased the nerves I didn't know were present until I saw her warm face.

'How can I help you?' she said.

I sat on the chair to the right of her desk, noting the photograph of her, a man and two children: a girl and a boy, assuming they were her family. They looked happy. I swallowed back the irritation I felt knowing hers was dynamically very different to mine.

'I've been having dreams, nightmares really. Some things have happened recently. Things I'd rather not go into detail about. Criminal. Not me, someone close, and I thought it might have been related, but I've been having them on and off for years and they've become intrusive.'

'So, they've returned, these nightmares? And you think recent events have triggered them?'

'Yes. But it's not just the nightmares. It's what they involve, and I think they might relate to something that happened to me as a girl.'

'Childhood trauma can express itself during certain times of our lives. When did they begin?'

'When my youngest son was four years old. The thing is, aside from these nightmares I think are memories, I have none.'

'You can't remember certain things from your childhood?'

'No. I have no memory of my childhood at all except for the dreams. And even then, I can't rely on them as being factual, can I? If I've nothing to compare them to.'

'These nightmares, what do they consist of?'

'Aliens. Abduction. I've read about false memory syndrome, but I can't find anything in existence that could explain why I wake thinking I'm lying on a

271

hospital bed in a sterile steel room. And the lights, they're blinding.'

'I can see from your notes you suffered a difficult birth with your eldest son, Iefan?'

'You think that's where it stems from?'

'I'm not a psychiatrist, but it could be related.'

'I had a natural birth though there were complications. They thought I might need an emergency caesarean. I wasn't put to sleep in the end. Rhys was delivered by ventrose. But in my nightmares, when I wake up, I can't move, almost as though I've been anesthetised.'

'Sleep paralysis can exhibit similar signs.'

'But how do you explain the lights, and The Shadow Man?'

'I can't,' she smiled sadly. 'Our dreams can represent an array of things. Researchers are still attempting to explain how REM sleep works as opposed to daydreaming. I'm afraid I'm not going to be able to help you interpret them. How are you sleeping, generally?'

'Fine, I guess, until all this stuff with my father. I've always been a light sleeper, but I could drift off okay.'

I could see from her eyes she'd already assessed

the relevance of my father, the crime, my childhood amnesia, and my recently triggered nightmares, formulating an evaluation from the facts just as I had.

'And how are you feeling generally?' she said, eyeing my notes on-screen.

'I was shocked, at first. Then angry. And I suppose sad. But I'm not depressed.'

'You don't have a history of mental illness in the family?' she said.

'No.'

*Not unless your father molesting you counts.*

'I can offer you an appointment with a counsellor. The referral process can take approximately three to four months I'm afraid. But you can speak to the Psychological Wellbeing Practitioner before your initial consultation to give your allocated therapist some information about your background. The NHS offer up to eight sessions free of charge. If you require further support, you can arrange that with your counsellor. Would that be something you would like to do?'

I looked at the door, to where on the other side my husband sat waiting for me to leave there with, if not a solution, then at least a point in the right direction.

'Yes. Please.'

I left the building with Lewis at my heel. Rather than take the car straight home, we slunk off to a café where we were met with the strong scent of rich, bitter coffee. Mine was topped with cream and coated with a thin dusting of cocoa. A neighbouring child swung on his chair and squealed. My hand gripped the glass cup firmly as I took a swig of the hot sweet caramel latte.

As I shifted in my chair the folded pieces of paper, printed off by the locum doctor rustled in the pocket of my jeans. Information on False Abduction Syndrome, a recently researched phenomenon where individuals dream about and become convinced that they've been abducted by aliens when in fact they've been sexually abused. Or at least that's what I concluded from reading just the abstract as I perched on the toilet seat in the bathroom of the café to calm my racing heart while Lewis ordered the coffee.

I stared through the window, gazing at the bruised coloured sky, wondering where spring had gone when a familiar chime cut through the humdrum of murmured conversations surrounding me. My phone rang from somewhere inside my handbag. I answered without bothering to glance down at the screen to see who was calling. It took me a moment to recognise the glacial notes of Gwenda's hurried words, cutting deep into my flesh like a slashing knife.

'Has it arrived?'

'Has what arrived?'

'The diary. I forgot all about it. I sent it first class, so you should have received it today.'

I dashed out of the café, ignoring the tutting customers as I flew past their tables almost knocking precariously balanced cups from them and causing napkins to fly into the air as though I had caused a small hurricane, and lunged for the door before it closed behind a woman in front of me. When I stepped out onto the pavement, I finally exhaled the breath that had caught in my throat. I didn't want Lewis to witness my discomfort or overhear our conversation. 'You found my diary?'

'Yes. About five months ago. Before I looked you up online. I kept it safe in the cottage. But what with all this, what's been going on, it completely slipped my mind.'

'You posted it when?'

'Two days ago.'

The wind whistled as I crossed the street, past a sign, and down an alley toward the large gothic building of St Mary's chapel. The fork in the road somewhere behind me contained my husband, calling my name, wondering where I'd gone and why I'd left the café so hastily.

I found myself on bent knees facing the altar inside the large church, my blue skirt flayed out across the marble in the shape of a half-moon. The building was omnipresent. Lit brightly from above. Spacious, cool, silent. Lewis appeared at my side and asked me what I was doing there.

I glanced up at him, imagining Gwenda's green cat-like eyes glaring at me while she continued to speak. 'There's something I must tell you,' she said. 'Will you be coming back here before the house is sold?'

Lewis sank down beside me, and I lowered my voice, noting the elderly couple stood in the centre of the aisle ahead of us, staring up at the handcrafted decorative ceiling. 'I know what you did to Bryn. I worked it out days ago from what you insinuated. I'm not angry.'

'I don't regret it, though I know it makes me no better than him,' she said, choking on her own words.

When she next spoke, I felt the cold marble floor on my bare legs and the hand I used to hold the phone to my ear begin to tremble. 'It began with you, Carys.'

She was right. It did. My fathers abuse started with me and progressed over the years to the desire to fill the hollow in his life by snatching girls off the street.

'You read it.'

She didn't reply.

I thought of her flicking through the pages of my diary where, as a twelve-year-old child I wrote my darkest secrets.

'Where did you find it?'

'In your old bedroom.'

Lewis gave me a questioning stare that said, 'what are you discussing?'

I averted my eyes, ashamed she'd read my most intimate thoughts. Though I couldn't blame her for having the compulsion to do so.

'You think my father killed Siân?' I whispered.

'I know he did. And I won't rest until her body is found and I'm able to prove it.'

By the time I ended the call my mind was reeling.

Lewis took my arm and linked it through his, weaving me through a group of student-visa tourists in awe of an explanatory plaque above the dockside providing information on the cave gardens where pirates had supposedly stowed their wares delivered by ships via the gated stone entrance, as we ambled down the steps to where I slumped onto a wall overlooking the casino, staring at my feet.

'Who was it?' he asked.

'Gwenda.'

'What did she want?'

'She sent a parcel. My diary.'

Then I told him what Gwenda had said before she'd cut the call.

'She poisoned your father?'

'With ephedrine. Apparently, it causes a rush of adrenaline the heart can't cope with.'

'Let's go for a walk along the docks?' said Lewis, trying to process my words.

I breathed in the smoggy fumes and nodded.

'You can't keep this to yourself. You have to tell the police,' he said, when we found a quiet spot. 'She killed your father.'

'She wants to talk. To meet with me. Explain.'

'She's a murderer,' he scoffed.

I nodded my ascent, but I knew I had to hear her

out, no matter how irrelevant the things she needed to offload.

If anything offered a clue to the whereabouts of Siân or could uncover Seren's long ago decomposed remains the chance to resolve the past might pave the way for me to begin a clean-slated future.

We returned to the car half an hour later. Lewis navigated out of the tight parking space and reversed away from the doctor's surgery.

I sat staring out of the passenger window at the historical buildings, road-block traffic, hurried businessmen and women in suits returning home from their corporate jobs. And I felt a stirring of compassion for the woman who'd tricked my father, although it scared me a little.

When we arrived home our neighbour was already halfway down the path of her neat semi-detached house that housed a normal family, holding out the brown, paper-wrapped, book-shaped parcel I knew contained the diary I hadn't seen in twenty-four years. As I took it from her outstretched hand I felt the private accusations inside it burn my palm.

# RHIANNON

*Brynmawr, Ebbw Vale, Wales, 1995*

Rhiannon lay in bed, head spinning, the words she'd read several hours before enlarging and rotating before her eyes. She knew she should have taken her pills to curb the unquenchable thirst and hallucinations that plagued her when her blood-sugar level was too high but what was the point. She'd spent her entire life living with a man she couldn't trust to be alone with her own daughter, did everything she could to separate them, had resigned from a decent job with a good income to stay at the farm, to please God, her husband, and Carys. Thinking Bryn was the problem and that God would remove from him the lustrous temptations he could not control. And all along they were deceiving her, laughing at her behind her back. Death would be a welcome release.

*Dear Diary,*

*I saw B today. He waited for me outside the school gate. We watched cartoons together then he sat me on his lap and like all the other times I felt butterflies. Mother would kill us if she found out, but he promised she won't.*

*Dear Diary,*

*I was in a bad mood, so B bought me sweets. He gave me a cuddle and I felt myself melt in his arms. I wonder if that's what love feels like?*

She'd birthed the bitch, and this was how Carys repaid her.

Rhiannon's vision blurred as she stood. She gripped the bedside unit and hauled herself up. She crossed the bedroom toward the door, heard Bryn snoring from beneath the sheets.

It wasn't too late to turn things round. Bryn had only sunk his claws into her so far. Carys was a resilient girl. She'd meet a boy her own age and realise how wrong it was to love her father in a romantic way.

She stumbled down the stairs, popped two pills into her mouth, and wandered the house aimlessly. Restless, fired up, she crept back upstairs and into Carys' light pink painted bedroom.

How could she sleep with a guilty conscience?

She stood in the doorway, reminiscing over the first years they'd shared, now tarred with the knowledge that Carys would grow up to steal her own father from his wife, the mother who'd fed, clothed, washed, and comforted her.

Who was Rhiannon if not a wife and mother?

What was her purpose if she lost both her husband and daughter?

# CARYS

*Redland, Bristol, England, 2018*

I arranged the photographs in order of significance, but there were gaps on the table where the girls should be, and spaces where pictorially their lives had ended. It was no good. I couldn't do it. It felt too personal. Morbid. Wrong. I shoved my chair back and walked the length of the room, leant over the table with my damp palms on the melamine. It wasn't the girls I should be focusing on. It was me.

The counselling sessions were due to start in five weeks. The PWP who'd called me the day before had given me a cancellation. It meant I might finally discover how to deal with the things that affected my mind on a nightly basis.

Iefan crossed the dining room, put his arms around me and sank his head onto my shoulder. I patted his head. In unspoken words he said, 'I'm here for you, mum.'

I fought back tears, for the girl I'd once been. The naivety of the children my father had hurt, their innocence destroyed. And for the defenceless infant who hadn't asked to be brought into this world but had died before taking her first breath in it.

I watched Iefan retreat into the dimly lit hallway, heard him enter the kitchen, open the fridge and the image of the putrid yellow walls of the kitchen inside my childhood home fluttered in front of my eyes, blurring the boundary between the present and past.

My mind drifted back to one summer on the farm, when Bryn had burnt the corn to cinder. 'It's no good. Rotten,' he said, stood in front of the back door that led from the kitchen and out onto the lawn.

I felt those words on my skin, hard and hot. 'She's rotten. No good. Wicked girl,' said my father, about Zoe. 'Flaunting her feminine beauty, wearing makeup, and staying out past curfew.'

Zoe was working in London these days, for some big publisher. I'd looked her up when I heard the news. DI Locke had travelled the one hundred and fifty miles to interview her, to confirm some details her father had given Detective Murrow during the initial stages of the investigation into Seren's disappearance. Information concerning several members of the community he thought might be worth them checking out.

The police had also recently questioned Zoe's father, Frank's, whereabouts on the day of the girls' disappearances. Frank had an alibi and a witness. But he could not account for the connection they'd made between his friends, Joe Sykes and Bill Erwin.

Joe was Gwenda's ex-boyfriend, Siân's father.

According to the police, Joe had committed suicide in the garage of their Abergavenny house less than a year after their daughter was reported missing. He was working in Ebbw Vale the day of Seren's disappearance, and he owned a navy-blue car.

I didn't think Joe was responsible for taking his own daughter, but the police, and it seemed the reporters, found it suspicious that Frank had been driving Joe Sykes' car that day.

The article I'd read online stated that an anonymous child witness had come forward to say he'd seen Siân being bundled into a blue car at around 4:30pm the day she'd vanished. The same car that Frank had collected and delivered to Bill the week before.

Now an adult, Kian had come forward to speak to DI Locke, had given her a sketch of the man he recognised. The picture resembled Bill Erwin, who'd been arrested at his home address earlier that morning.

Neither Frank nor Joe were Jehovah's Witnesses, although Gwenda and Emma, their partners, were. As was my mother.

The connection didn't end there. The men spent a lot of their free time together. Bill was a car salesman. Joe was an auto-electrician, and often travelled from Abergavenny to fix the vehicles Bill sold from the garage he ran in Ebbw Vale. Frank collected cars from the auction in Bristol or Newport, or from private sellers for Bill to re-sell. The ones he couldn't were retrieved from Frank and taken to his scrapyard in Pontypool. Situated three roads away from where my father's vehicle had been discovered burnt out after it was stolen by the two youths the police were in the process of interviewing to determine the relevance of the information they'd learned.

Frank, Joe, and Bill were self-employed. They'd

also each given one another alibis, their police statements identical. Only Franks could be verified.

After a re-interview and some gentle persuasion to tell the truth, honesty being one of the biblical commandments he was supposed to adhere to, and which I assumed the police had reminded him of, Bill had confirmed Detective Murrow's earlier suspicions to the 'detective in charge' who I knew as DI Locke, according to the journalist's interpretation of the ongoing case, updated hourly on the Wales Online article which I'd read fifteen minutes before.

Bill had been in Abergavenny when Siân had disappeared. Joe had been in Ebbw Vale when Seren had been reported missing. Ella's abduction appeared to be an anomaly. With a few clicks of the cursor I discovered that Bill was currently being held in custody pending further enquiries.

Did that mean Frank Culver, Joe Sykes, and Bill Erwin knew Stephen Lloyd, Seren's father, and Matthew James, Ella's father?

And if they were all collectively responsible for planning and executing the girl's abductions, rapes, and murders, where did Bryn Howell, my own father, fit in?

# BRYN

*Brynmawr, Ebbw Vale, Wales, 1993*

Bryn opened the front door to his oldest friend, Bill Erwin, with a tumbler in one hand ready to pour him a glass of whiskey.

Rhiannon was in Newport, had taken the car to travel to Gwent Royal where she took blood from patients. It wasn't a well-paid job, but she enjoyed getting out of the house and away from the farm. It gave Bryn time to work in his study upstairs and to meet his closest ally. Bill was also his alibi in case anything went wrong. Which it had when he'd let the girl go. He vowed never to let that happen again.

Bryn knew getting caught was a possibility, but with Bill's help he could wheedle his way out of a problem much easier.

'Where is she?' said Bill, taking a seat on the other

end of the sofa.

'In the basement.'

'You're keeping her?'

'Until I've had enough of her.'

Bill had brought the girl to him the morning before. But he couldn't let her go. He hadn't finished with her yet.

'Do you want a go?'

He nodded. 'I'll have my whiskey first.'

Frank had no idea that the cars he delivered to Bill had been used to abduct the girls. The first – Catherine – had struggled so violently she'd managed to get her inside the vehicle. He waited for the police to turn up since her escape, but when they didn't, he decided she must have kept her mouth shut. Which meant he could continue for as long as he chose. Or until he got caught. Whichever came sooner.

Bryn was careful. He always wore gloves, had the vehicles valeted before handing them back to Frank who brought them to the dealership for Bill to sell. The only place where any evidence of his illicit activities remained was in the basement no one could get into without his key.

After downing the last mouthful of his whiskey,

Bill stood and turned toward the living room door.

'Go easy on her,' said Bryn. 'She's not as feisty as Catherine was.'

Bryn knew that suited Bill fine. He liked them young because they were less inclined to cause trouble. Bryn though, picked them. They had to have rose blonde hair and pale skin. Like his daughter, Carys.

Bill had remarked on it once, but he pretended he had no idea what he was insinuating. Bill said he didn't really care, but it made Bryn question what it was about her that caused the desire he had difficulty articulating, least of all excusing. He supposed it had something to do with his wife.

Rhiannon had been slim, attractive, wavy haired, and feminine. Before Carys was born. She used to joke that their daughter had stolen her looks and he had to admit the accusation sounded plausible. From the moment she grew old enough to go to school, Bryn's feelings toward Carys shifted from fatherly love to an obsession he couldn't stop obsessing about.

Bill must have sensed something within him, because it was Bill who'd suggested he take Catherine. And it was Bill who'd brought the one currently residing in the basement with him the day before. They'd never spoken to each other about their hobby, but somehow both knew it was something they enjoyed. And it wasn't as though they were harming anyone was it?

At least that's what Bryn told himself, at first. Until he heard Bill's footsteps echoing up the concrete steps of the basement, looking frustrated and hot. 'She's gone.'

Bryn jumped off the sofa and moved toward the doorway at speed. 'What do you mean *gone*?'

Bill made a slashing knife across the throat sign with his fat forefinger. 'You're going to have to get rid of her or she's going to stink out the farm.'

'You killed her?'

Bill looked stunned by his question. Then he said, 'what else was I supposed to have done with her? You've had your fun. I've had mine. Now we can't afford to get locked up for this can we?'

He shook his head. He knew Bill was right, but he hadn't expected such a calm, controlled man to be so ruthless as to end a young child's life. A girl only two years older than his eleven-year-old daughter, Carys.

'What am I supposed to do with her?'

Bill laughed and pointed down the hall to the kitchen where the back door led out onto the garden. 'Bury her. You've got plenty of land. No one saw me bring her here. No one's going to suspect either of us of anything.'

Bryn took a deep breath and walked down the hall toward the open basement door. He trod down the steps into the cold room and saw the girl. Amelia, she said her name was. She was led on the mattress, her pale-yellow Tammy Girl dress with the orange flowers printed all over it still tied around her throat.

He took a deep breath and descended the final few steps, his eyes on the girl, her beautiful pale face turning purple around her chin where her blood supply had been severed. She hadn't felt pain, just the gasping breath and the knowledge she was about to die before she closed her eyes and fell into a dark and heavy sleep. Like the animals on the farm when they'd sucked in their final breath. Amelia was no different to a runt lamb, he told himself as he neared her.

He stood a while staring at her perfectly formed features, dainty hands, fingers curled as though she'd bunched her hands into fists. He looked back at Bill stood in the doorway at the top of the steps. He didn't wear any defence marks his wife would see when he returned home. Not that his wife would notice. She was too consumed with her prognosis to worry about what her husband might be up to when he disappeared for hours. But Rhiannon would know something was wrong unless he covered up his friend's crime quickly.

'Go and grab me a sheet from the linen cupboard upstairs so I can wrap her up. She'll be easier to carry then.'

Bill moved slowly as though he didn't have a care in the world. He returned with a fresh-scented white sheet and tossed it down to Bryn who caught it, threw it over the girl, turned her onto her front and wrapped the sheet around her. He tied both ends to ensure she didn't fall out as he hoisted her body up and over his shoulder to carry her out of the farm.

Bill grabbed a spade that was leaning against the barn wall and followed Bryn.

With precision Bill dug a deep hole in the ground beneath some bracken laden from the surrounding ferns in the undergrowth of the woods. As far away from the farm as they could go, but close enough that

Bryn could see the area from his side of the wall where the pig sty was situated.

The council owned the land, but no one bothered to cross that patch, so he knew Amelia's body would be safe from discovery. And within fifteen minutes, she lay below the earth where he hoped no one would ever find her.

# CARYS

*Redland, Bristol, England, 2018*

Following the news was becoming a habit I couldn't withdraw from. It was like watching a medical programme. I wanted to look, but with one eye closed to the horror.

Bill Erwin had been released on bail pending further enquiries. His ill health had given the Crown Prosecution Service cause for concern regarding his ability to cope with prison life due to his age, and the possibility other inmates might harm him due to the seriousness of the crimes they suspected him of if he was held on remand. Offences which they wouldn't divulge, but I could guess were related to his involvement in the abductions and murders of The Girls as the reporters now called them. Because no one really knew how many of them there were.

He wasn't considered an immediate threat to the public's safety, nor did the detectives believe he was a flight risk. He didn't own a passport and had handed over his driving licence to the DVLA after his involvement in a near fatal collision the previous autumn. The article mentioned the incident as 'age related careless driving.' The surviving male victim of the crash had made a full recovery though both vehicles were written off. But looking at Bill on the short video that had just been released online as he was being bundled into the back of an unmarked police car with a newspaper over his head, ironically covering his face with his own on the front page, as he left Cardiff Magistrates Court for home, I saw what others couldn't.

In the stooped over, grey-haired man I saw the kind, friendly version of Bill who'd let me into his house to play cards when my father had failed to collect me from school. I saw the man who sat opposite my father at the dinner table eating the food my mother had cooked after his wife had died. I saw the man who'd sold my father his red MG after the two youths had stolen and burnt the light blue car the police weren't able to discover any evidence on to prove it had been used for anything other than riding down maximum speed country roads. I saw the man I knew had crushed that same vehicle, and according to the detectives, the other vehicles they suspected Bryn had used to abduct The Girls.

I had a hard time merging the two versions of Bill into one whole. Just as I had as a teen with my father.

It looked increasingly likely that Bryn and Bill had worked together. Supplier and enabler. But as so much time had passed and there was no concrete proof to confirm DI Locke's theory that Bill had abused the girls whose remains were yet to be discovered on my father's property that now unfortunately belonged to me, they had to release him.

I stood on shaking legs and walked toward the landline, picked up the receiver, and dialled the number I hadn't realised I remembered until I heard the call connecting. I slammed the phone down the second I heard his voice. Bill Erwin might have looked different, but he sounded the same.

I slumped down onto the bottom of the staircase and gazed at the phone in my hand, wondering what remained of the Bill I'd grown up thinking as a confidant when things at home were difficult during my teen years. Had time eroded that man, or had he never really been there to begin with?

I knew one thing for certain. Bill was involved in my father's sinful lusts and I had been ignorant of that fact until I'd learned of his arrest. His subsequent release felt like a double blow to the back of my head.

# SEREN

*Brynmawr, Ebbw Vale, Wales, 1994*

Seren followed Bryn through the cool dark woods. The overhanging wisps of cottonwood branches dangled in front of her and brushed against her face as she inched slowly through the trees.

She was weak, hadn't eaten in days, felt her stomach lurch as she heard the cracking twigs beneath her light footsteps. Her heart was pounding and the air surrounding her felt as though it was weighted with thrumming danger. Her skin prickled with unease as though she'd caught her dress on the electric wire fence that separated the lawn from the paddock they'd passed. She wanted to flee but knew she wouldn't get far. She'd given up struggling. It only led him to punish her.

Bryn's grip tightened around her forearm as they

ambled through the bracken and into a narrow clearing where through the brush, she could see a wide stretch of grass.

With freedom in her grasp she stumbled, staring straight ahead, pulse quickening as her feet fell one at a time, pulled this way and tugged that way until at last they were facing a stream that curved around the foothill. Dandelions and shrubbery met the reeds on the waterbed to her right. The woodland trees stood sentry on the other side. Bryn seemed trancelike, watching the gentle current push stones and twigs along at his feet where he stood to her left.

The stream was shallow but muddy, and the bank slippery. She thought if he pushed her headfirst into the current and held her down, she'd gag on minnows and slimy weeds before she drowned.

He stepped forward so that she was stood two feet behind him, close enough to stretch her hands out and shove him into the water. It might not halt him for long, it wasn't deep. But with just the right amount of shock he could stumble and fall in, soak his feet and the bottoms of his trousers and it might stall his chase long enough for her to make it through the parting she could see ahead of her, into the woods where she could hide until dusk.

He must have sensed her cunning, for he turned at that exact moment and sneered. 'Don't even think about it, Seren. You're far too knowledgeable, I have got to end this the right way. With you gone nobody will know I took you.'

He was right of course, nobody had seen her slide willingly onto the rear passenger seat of his blue car. She'd been missing for three days, and already the streets were starting to clear of searchers, and rescue services were slowly dispersing home to their own families to await the news that her body had been discovered. She was determined that if her corpse was found something of hers would be left to alert the police where she'd been. But the land surrounding Bryn's four-acre farm was unused by dog walkers, fishermen, hikers, or children choosing to bunk off school. If she left anything behind Bryn would find it and get rid of it, just as he intended to do with her. She had no choice but to accept her fate.

A sound, in the distance, drew their attention to a tractor slowly pushing aside hay in a nearby field. The motor of the large machine cutting and slicing. The sound set her nerves on edge. The driver wasn't close enough for her to raise her arms in the air and yell to gain his attention but was within sight, and it forced Bryn to grow anxious they might be seen.

She took her chance, kicked him hard in the groin as her father had shown her to do if she felt threatened by a predatory male, something she wished she'd had the confidence to do before, and he folded, clutching his lower regions.

She pushed him hard in the chest then stood back and saw concern flit across his eyes.

She kicked him again, but he lashed out this time, catching her off-guard and splitting her cheek with the band on his wedding finger. Blood sprayed across his shirt, spotting the light beige fabric with dots of claret. The colour of the wine her mother liked to drink when her father was away driving lorries across the country.

Only Seren knew Stephen was visiting his fancy woman. They'd spoken once on the phone when she'd answered for him by mistake. He growled at her and ripped the receiver from her hand, but she couldn't pretend she hadn't heard the woman on the other end of the line breathe a smoky, 'honey, I miss you.'

Her mother was unaware of her husband's affair

and Seren didn't want to split her family up, so she kept quiet. She was good at keeping secrets.

But in that moment, staring into the evil eyes of her captor she could hold her silence no more. She released a deafening screech before she ran as fast as she could back toward the undergrowth, determined she would survive to tell the tale of her seventy-two-hour abduction.

Panting, tired, muscles aching as they stretched, and with her heart thudding hard beneath her ribs as she felt a tightening band of adrenaline push her forward, she imagined she'd taken flight like a bird, soaring through the sky to flee the mighty eagle chasing his prey.

# CARYS

*Redland, Bristol, England, 2018*

I learned that afternoon as I soaked in the bath with the latest copy of Good Housekeeping spread open on the sink in my tiny bathroom I had a hard job reading from as I soaked in rose scented, moisturising bubble bath that the skeleton of a girl had been found near the woods set back several yards from the disused cornfield surrounding the paddock near to where Ella's remains had been exhumed eighteen days prior.

I felt sick to my stomach and exited the bath to dress hastily, not bothering with a towel, the phone slipping from my soapy fingers, the screen hitting the tiles and shattering at my feet.

Rhys was attending the college open day with his father. I didn't want my personal drama to potentially disrupt a discussion between him and one of his future tutors. I thought about calling Iefan, but he was with his girlfriend and was intending to meet up with Rhys and the girl he'd been dating for the past four months in Bella Italia followed by bowling and possibly a movie in less than an hour. I couldn't disturb him either. I should have called Lewis, but instead I dressed quickly and spoke to Gwenda from the landline in the living room while I tried to reassemble my splintered thoughts.

We'd grown close in the days since her unexpected phone call, to inform me she'd sent the parcel containing the diary, scrawled with my childish handwriting.

After a walk around the docks Lewis and I had gone for a pot of tea in a cosy little pub facing the harbourside, leaving before the rush of four-day workers wanting to get drunk before returning to their student digs or commuting home. I called Gwenda the moment we returned home, before retreating upstairs alone where I skim-read a few pages from the diary. When I reached the part about my bedtimes I threw it against the wall, unable to cope with the images that plagued me.

I learned more from Gwenda. She knew my

mother. Had never met my father until she had befriended him for the tidy sum of fifteen thousand pounds that she felt he owed her.

She knew Bryn had killed her daughter because he drove a blue car around the time that Siân had gone missing. 'There was a sighting, not reported on by the newspaper, the day she disappeared. The police didn't pursue it- unreliable testimony.'

I knew the name of the man who'd once lived with his parents on the same road as Gwenda as a boy was Kian, the thirty-two-year-old who'd come forward to re-report his sighting of the vehicle to the police when he'd heard about the excavation of my father's land. The inheritance of which I still struggled to accept was mine.

I stared at the phone in my hand before dialling. Gwenda answered the call with a croaky voice. She'd been crying. 'The remains . . . It's my Siân. I know it is.'

I allowed her to cry it out, the years of emotional strife left her unable to speak properly through the tears that kept on falling, even as I placed the receiver down, promising to call her later.

She'd heard about the bones discovered just past the old pig sty that was no more. I knew the square foot space like the back of my hand because my father often threatened to feed me to them when I'd been naughty.

'They eat little girls for breakfast,' he said.

I yawned, my eyes filling with tears.

I'd done a lot of reading overnight. According to what I briefly skimmed over, archaeologists use ground penetrating radar that collects and records images of items below the earth. The ones being used on the four acres of land had swept the entire perimeter until they'd come across the remains of what was presumed to be a teenage female buried deep beneath the clay soil where nothing grew. The part-clothed skeleton and nearby mud particles were taken to a lab for examination.

The farm had been sealed off for three weeks. The once flat garden, paddock and the field beyond where my father had at one time, when I was young, kept several sheep to graze so he wouldn't have to mow the lawn with the land-runner, was now a mass of clumped earth. Mounds of it according to Gwenda. It would take several weeks for a landscaper to go over it all and spread grass seeds on the bare soil. It looked likely we'd have to wait until September before we could return there, and with the amount of work that needed doing we'd have to cut back on expenses. The thought of staying in the house where my father had hidden two girls and a baby was unfortunate but having to face the senile spinster who'd birthed one of them and had admitted to poisoning my father because she quite rightly suspected him of murdering her daughter, was far worse.

The experts had exhausted their resources after widening the expanse of their search and unless Seren's remains could be located soon there would be no area left on the property to dig up. Gwenda was either in shock or relieved, knowing at least the remains of who she suspected was her daughter had been found because she spoke in a detached tone while reiterating all this.

A part of me knew it was irrational, but I felt as though I should apologise to her, and to Ella's parents, for my father's crimes. If I'd known what Bryn was up to, I could have done something to prevent him from taking those girls. If only I'd have been his sacrificial lamb, then maybe neither of them would have died.

Lewis tried to reason with me, stating that I was just a child myself when Seren, who the police believed to have been the second abductee was taken, whose bones had not been found. None of the robotic lenses scoping the land had dislodged a trace of her, but that didn't mean she wasn't there, somewhere.

After her parent's divorce, Seren's father, Stephen, had moved to Leeds with the tart he'd been sleeping with behind his wife's back while she had opened several more hair salons managing the spread of them throughout Gwent and setting up her own training school. I'd looked her up. She seemed to have moved on incredibly well for a woman whose daughter had gone missing less than two decades prior and whose dress had recently been discovered in what the newspapers were now calling The Murder House. Her daughter, who until recently, had been presumed alive. The man currently suspected responsible for her death unable to pay for his sins.

Then I imagined Gwenda poisoning him and thought that perhaps he had.

# SEREN

*Brynmawr, Ebbw Vale, Wales, 1994*

Bryn shoved Seren hard and it threw her off balance. She landed face-first at the streams edge. She looked up, and on all fours tried to stand as she faced the rippling water, where a group of gnats circled a clump of rocks that jutted out of it. Bryn stooped over her with his arms outstretched to wrap his hands around her throat from behind. She ducked and struggled to crawl away, her elbows burning against the coarse grass as he dragged her up and pulled her backwards until she lay on the ground, her spine digging into the swollen, cracked soil.

Raising her legs and kicking him ferociously until he backed away, he stumbled, releasing her throat a little so that she could draw in some air, but he scooted to her side and remained on all fours above her, snarling like a vicious dog.

He lunged, ferociously and pounced on her. Again, his hands found their way to her throat, but this time he was undeterred. He squeezed, tighter this time, his thumbs digging into her larynx and adding enough pressure to make her feel sick and grow dizzy.

She could see madness in his dark eyes before the edges of her vision blurred and she began to see black sludges in front of her. 'You need to go,' he said, over and again.

She gasped in one final lungful of air, but panting, exhausted, and weak from having eaten barely a thing in days she soon grew too tired to defend herself, and eventually her hands, trembling around his while her eyes pleaded with him to stop strangling her, fell slack. He shrugged off her loose grip, pulled away and closed her eyes to prevent her accusing stare from putting him off getting rid of her body.

He swung round to face the sty several yards away then looked back across the thin inlet of the river to where he'd buried Amelia, contemplating where to dispose of Seren.

# CARYS

*Redland, Bristol, England, 2018*

I drove on autopilot to the studio where I'd not been in days. I couldn't face seeing the photographs I'd taken of the place I'd once called home, mounted on stilts, facing the door. The farm, the place that was now infested with reporters from all over the country, rooting through confessional interviews from neighbours, some of whom hadn't even lived in Ebbw Vale during my childhood, nor knew my father, but who seemed to have plenty to say about the man they'd never met.

'I always had a feeling about that house. There was something not right about it,' said one woman who'd retired to the town five years before.

'He was a private man, but his eyes were black as coal,' said one man, who'd worked with Bryn Howell at the accountancy firm before he'd transferred the business premises to his home address. Her description was probably the only one that resembled anything close to the truth, compared to the other quotes printed in that morning's edition of the Ebbw Vale News.

Franks interview was contradictory. On the one hand he'd described my father as a 'hard-working family man with good morals' but in the same paragraph stated, 'this proves no one really knew him.' He also supposed 'anyone is capable of anyhting' and 'if they deny responsibility as well as Bryn must have, even to themselves, they aren't capable of empathy or remorse.'

I jumped at the sound of the landline ringing. The only people who had my work number was Lewis, who wouldn't call the studio unless there was an emergency, Sharon who was no expected back to work until Monday, and DI Locke. I gathered it was the latter and held my breath to await more bad news.

'Amelia Holbrooke, age thirteen, reported missing in June 1993 from Cwmbran shopping centre has been positively identified using DNA-indexing from the remains discovered in the woodland near to where the pig sty was situated.'

I released an anguished sigh.

'Carys?'

'Yes, I'm still here. I just . . . I don't know what to say . . . I feel so . . .'

*Empty. Lost. Scared. Lonely. Sad.*

'I understand this is incredibly difficult for you. But I have to inform you at each stage so that everyone is on the same page.'

'Yes, I know. It's just that . . .'

Should I tell her that Gwenda murdered my father?

*No*, said my conscience. *He deserved to die after what he did.* Another voice entered my head then and said, *so does Bill.*

'This is all so . . .'

'There's a bit of a media storm here, Carys, so I-'

'You have to go, I understand.'

'But if you do need to-'

'Talk to you? I will detective. And thank you for keeping me updated.'

'If there is anything-'

'I'll call you.'

I hung up feeling winded.

It was all coming out and I was worried about what else might arise.

# BRYN

*Brynmawr, Ebbw Vale, Wales, 1994*

Bryn left the river, crossed the field along the entrance to the woods past the sty, took lengthy strides through the paddock, and entered the barn to collect the spade which hung on a nail over the circular table saw. Bracken and snapping twigs crunched beneath the soles of his boots as he hurried away from the farm, returning to the scene of his crime. There, he entered a copse of trees and began to dig.

He stood a while, looking at the shallow pit of earth where he planned to dump Seren. His earlier exhilaration replaced with an element of satisfaction for a job almost complete as his adrenaline began to wane, leaving his racing pulse to thrum evenly throughout his body.

He trundled back toward the clearing, to where he'd left Seren lying on the ground, but he didn't hear Carys tiptoe through the field.

She smiled nervously when he turned on her, blood draining from his face.

'What's the matter father?'

Not wanting her to detect the worry he felt in that moment he downplayed his symptoms and smiled weakly, hoping his eyes had deceived him and the ground still held the body of Seren he mistakenly perceived was vacant.

'How long have you been standing there for?'

'Long enough.'

'What did you see?'

She didn't reply, but instead pointed back to the house. 'Mother's home. She wants to talk to you.'

'How did you . . . get here? I mean, did she pick you up from school?'

Carys shook her head, eyes drawn to the spade he held in one hand, his other clenched into a tight fist at his side. 'I walked.'

'Go on into the house. I'll follow.'

She paused a moment, a flicker of concern evident on her face that caused him suddenly to become wary.

The moment she turned toward the house he glanced back at the clearing, shook his head, and ran a hand through his receding hairline.

Seren was gone.

# CARYS

*Redland, Bristol, England, 2018*

I sat across from the woman I'd spoken to on the phone the day before, confirming my appointment. She listed a long inventory of qualifications and specialisms, but what I really wanted to know was how I could stop the unbearable nightmares. I knew I couldn't rewind the clock and go back in time to stop any of the things that had happened to me over the course of my lifetime, but if I could find a way to combat the dread of going to sleep with the light off perhaps Lewis could lie beside me in the dark. As it was, I had taken to sleeping in the living room on the sofa with the television on mute, scaring Iefan and his girlfriend half to death when they returned together the night they'd gone with Rhys to the cinema, finding me comatose having taken three Zopiclones my GP had prescribed me while I waited for the first of eight standardised sessions with the Cognitive Behavioural Therapist seated three feet in front of me.

She wore a pair of tight fitted gunmetal grey jeggings and a black high-neck vest top. She looked ten years younger than me but when I enquired her age, she told me she was two years older than my thirty-six years.

She'd read my notes, knew my story, had listened to me drop bombshell after bombshell down the line during my telephone consultation, and attended patiently as I reiterated the same information to her face-to-face ten minutes ago. She wasn't a diagnostician, but she agreed with the locum's pre-emptive assessment: that I was suffering False Abduction Syndrome, and symptoms of complex Post-Traumatic Stress Disorder, which was mostly affecting my sleep.

'Wakefulness doesn't appear to be a problem for you?'

'No.'

*Not unless you think hearing the voice of your younger self blathering on at you all day constitutes as a dysfunction.*

'I've worked with many individuals experiencing PTSD. Adult survivors of child sexual abuse, and sleep difficulties. But I must admit I've not actually worked with anyone who presents with FAS, so I must inform you I may need to refer you on to a specialist.'

'You can't help me?'

'I can certainly teach you some techniques that could help you to relax and suggest some ways you could alter your night-time routine so that you can hopefully sleep without resorting to a medicinal aid but in my experience, you'd benefit from working with a psychotherapist over a longer period. Helping you to manage your symptoms is unlikely to assist you in learning to cope with the deeper issues that's causing them.'

I huffed. 'Don't you think I've already been using visualization exercises, squirting my pillow with lavender oil, taking warm baths surrounded with scented candles before going to bed? None of it has worked.'

'I understand those things aren't helping, which is why I think you'd gain more from the therapeutic process if you spoke to a specialist counsellor, over a longer term.'

'I don't want to go over the details about my private life with a stranger if I don't even feel comfortable enough expressing those things to my husband. I just want the fucking aliens to leave me the hell alone, so I can get some sleep.'

I stood on stiff legs, irritated and defiant with tears pooled in my eyes I didn't know were there until she reached out to me with a box of tissues that had been beside her on the small faux oak table.

Her kind offering released the dam. I shoved the tissue against my nose, grabbed my handbag from the floor, and left the room, unwilling to admit everything she'd said made sense. I needed help. Support she was unable to provide. She'd thrown me a line and I'd chucked the fish at her face.

I was too embarrassed to turn back. I flew down the stairs of the smart Clifton Psychological Wellness Centre where psychotherapists and hypnotherapists of all persuasions worked with people like me, and trudged down the steep steps onto the pavement, where suddenly my surroundings reconfigured.

I was in the basement. The cold air emanating from the Bristol docks a mile down the hill where I stood, pressing on my face. But I was no longer stood on the street metres from the building I'd just vacated with a distant view of Cabot Tower through the Sycamore trees between the houses. I was six years old, stood on the concrete floor of the damp basement. The white painted walls closing in on me. The steel grey Volkswagen cruising down the road was a filing cabinet parked in the corner of the otherwise near-empty room. The grille was a set of steel implements. The flash of car lights an indication of the fluorescent bulb beaming down on the hospital bed where The Shadow Man who walked toward me forced me to lie. My stiff limbs locked beneath starched clean sheets. My silver bracelet a leather strap binding my wrists. The man looming over me my abductor.

And then I saw it. I saw it all.

The metal gurney, the sharp steel dissecting equipment, and the stuffed owl that was still in the living room of my father's house. My mother's indifference toward me. Iefan's lack of genetic problems.

'Are you okay?' said a voice from above.

I blinked several times and I found myself cowering on the pavement, my arms wrapped tight around my legs drawn up to my chin.

I looked up into the eyes of a tall Asian man. His thick coarse beard decorating an awkward smile. 'Take my hand?' he said.

I did.

He helped me to stand, asked how I felt, if I was hurt.

'No, I'm fine. Just took a turn.'

He didn't look convinced when I thanked him and said I was going home, that I'd be okay. After several reassurances that I wasn't going to black out further down the road he reluctantly wished me well, turned, and walked slowly to his car parked a few metres down the hill. He glanced back at me several times to ensure I hadn't collapsed on the pavement before he got inside. He didn't start the engine until I'd walked to the end of the road and when he turned the corner, he gave me a wave. I nodded back to let him know I wasn't going to keel over and die on his watch.

I glanced at the screen of my newly purchased mobile phone. It was 1:15pm. I should have returned to the studio. The sign I'd left on the door declared I'd be *back in an hour*, but I didn't much feel like sorting through photographs of the place I'd occupied for sixteen years of my childhood if my theory was correct and Iefan wasn't my father's biological son.

I whizzed through my *contacts*, hit dial, and pressed the phone to my ear.

'DI Locke. The DNA you took from us. Does Iefan's match Rhys'?'

'What is this regarding, Carys?'

I didn't want to have to explain my reason for thinking what I did unless I had some other proof to back it up with.

'Did you search Bill's house?'

'Detectives did obtain a warrant to enter the property during his arrest and some items were taken for examination.'

Her vague answers gave me no clue as to what those items removed from his property might have been or how they had helped the police to determine it would be wise to release him on bail, though from the true crime dramas I used to enjoy watching before this real one began told me it was most probably his mobile phone and laptop.

'Does Bill have a basement?'

'I'd have to check with CSI. They drew a map of the property to show where the items were removed from.' She paused, added, 'can I ask what this is concerning?'

I debated lying. Then took a deep breath and said, 'I think Bill Erwin is Iefan's biological father. I think he abused me. I need to know if my son's DNA matches his to prove otherwise. I could pay for a test, but I thought as you've already taken swabs it would be quicker to ask you.'

'I'd need Iefan's consent before divulging such sensitive information-'

'Don't bother then.'

I hung up, feeling my head swirl with the possibility things weren't as simple as I'd assumed. It seemed every day brought more revelations. Each one slightly worse than the last. I wondered when it would end. Would I ever be free of the legacy left in the wake of my father's death?

My mobile phone shrilled on the passenger seat where I'd dropped it. I glanced down at the caller ID and hit *ignore*. If DI Locke wasn't going to help me then I'd have to do my own digging.

# BRYN

*Brynmawr, Ebbw Vale, Wales, 2018*

Bryn felt himself sway. His hearing became muffled, yet the sound of his heartbeat thudding an out of tune melody was all he could hear against the backdrop of his own struggle to inhale oxygen into his lungs. His legs gave out once more, and he sunk to the carpet, face red-hot from the exertion of fighting for breath.

He gasped, his chest tightening as though a belt had been tied around it and someone was tugging on the floppy end, restricting his airflow. He grasped onto the pinewood bedpost and pulled himself up from the floor a few inches at a time until he was stood holding it while he prayed for the first time in his life. 'Please God, don't let me die,' he panted. 'Not like this. Not now.'

This was payback. And he knew why.

He hadn't thought much about The Girls in so long he'd almost managed to pretend they weren't buried in various plots dotted about the farm and surrounding woodland that had remained an inherent piece of geography throughout over a century of his familial occupancy. But he never forgot their names.

Catherine never made it back to the farm. She'd run away the moment he opened the car door to get her inside. Amelia had been promised an ice cream and had gone with him willingly. But he suspected she had additional needs because she was far more trusting than the others and a little socially awkward. Ella came next. He told her that her mother had asked him to collect her from school. He got that wrong because she was an orphan and was living in a care home provided by social services. When he discovered her pregnancy, he decided to keep her and the infant in the basement. But fate had other ideas. The blessing of their deaths brought Seren. But like Catherine, she vanished. He stopped after that. But Bill kept finding them, invited him over to join in his depraved games. Eventually Bryn refrained from sharing The Girls with him and left him to his own devices. That was a mistake. He hadn't realised how sick and twisted Bill had become. Evil enough that he could take his own friend's daughter. Bryn was even more surprised to learn that Joe Sykes had provided him with an alibi for the day of Siân's disappearance. No wonder the man gassed himself. The guilt must have eaten him up inside. Like the maggots feasting on the rotting flesh of Joe and Gwenda's daughter buried below the re-concreted basement of Bill's taxidermist lab.

The sharp pain in his chest grew stronger. His neck had been stiff for hours, jaw aching for days, but he hadn't bothered to mention it to the doctor when she came to check his blood pressure, because that morning he'd woken up re-energised, as though the worrying symptoms he'd experienced had merely been a figment of his imagination. But it had returned, and now it hurt.

He crushed his fingers together into fists and stumbled around the bed. He caught a flash of plum coloured silk and heard the swish of a dress as his vision blurred. 'Rh . . . Rhiannon?'

He thought he'd seen her before. In the kitchen washing up as though her ghost haunted the rooms of the farmhouse.

'No Bryn. It's Gwenda.'

He looked up, caught a flush of frustration on her face. 'I told you to stay downstairs.'

'But I . . . I wanted . . .'

'No one cares what you're wearing. Grab my shoulder and we'll go down together.'

He didn't want to touch her. Didn't want her anywhere near him. Not after what she'd said to him. That the vitamin pills he'd been taking were in fact beta-blockers and Metformin. That she'd been slowly poisoning him for only she knew how long with the intention of killing him. But that it had been taking far longer than she'd prepared herself for.

'Come on, shift your feet. Go down and read your newspaper, eat your dinner, and I'll drop by tomorrow to see how you're doing. I've got to take Shadow to the vet at 5:30pm.'

She'd ripped the phone from the wall and taken the keys, locking up the entire house, including the windows, not that he had the strength to smash his way out of them. She hadn't said when he'd die but he felt his heart contracting ever more agonisingly. It wouldn't be long he suspected, depending of course on what she had planned to do to finally end his life.

Once she'd led him down the staircase into the living room and eased him onto the chair facing the television, he saw the syringe lying on the coffee table. He hadn't felt her latex gloved hands on his left arm as she'd assisted him down the stairs because for the past twenty minutes all he felt was a prickly sensation down his left arm.

He seized up, eyes roaming from the syringe to Gwenda's impassive face and back again. 'What are you going to do with that?' He knew it was a stupid question, but he wanted to hear her say the words aloud. If he could get her to talk it might give him time to gain enough strength to fight her off.

He tried to swallow but his throat was tight. A weight had descended on the centre of his chest and his mouth was dry. He wheezed, took in a lungful of air but it was increasingly harder to exhale.

'It's supposed to be pressed into your vein but it's going to be difficult to disguise a fresh needle mark, so I thought it would be better, although a lot more difficult, to put it through the wound where your GP took your bloods from this morning to test your iron levels. Though I don't suppose you're going to keep still for me, are you?'

He shook his head, but he lost his sight for a few moments, head swimming in a sea of pain.

He felt the prick of the needle and his eyes snapped open, his hand reached out to swipe the syringe from her fingers, but she pressed the heel of her shoe onto his sock covered toes and he gasped in shock as the liquid entered his vein.

The liquid felt cold as it worked its way up his shoulder, spreading like fire into his chest. He bent forward and gagged.

'No,' she said withdrawing the syringe carefully and dabbing at the fresh wound with a tissue which she stuffed into her pocket. 'We can't have you vomiting. That wouldn't do at all.'

He gritted his teeth as a wave of pain shot down his neck and into his chest. He gripped the arm of the chair and sank back clutching his tingling hand. His fingers had been numb for some time. The classic symptoms of an imminent heart attack he regretted ignoring.

'There you go,' said Gwenda, draping a blanket over his knobbly knees. His pyjama bottoms already soaked with urine.

Humiliated for having wet himself like Carys had many times as a child when she knew she was going to be punished, his hands trembled as he tried to grip the seam to throw the blanket off his sweaty body.

'You can't leave me here,' he choked, when she turned her back on him and moved several feet toward the door.

She spun round, leant forward over him, her nose inches from his own, looked him directly in the eyes, and said, 'I am going to wait until it's over then I will go home, grab Shadow, and walk him to the vet for *his* injection. But I very much would like to watch you take your last breath first.' She straightened herself, folded her arms, and remained standing several feet away, refusing to tear her gaze from him as he fought not to panic while he sucked in one more breath. One which this time he could not release. He shot her a look of what he hoped was anger, but knew must contain an element of fear, as pain spread from the pit of his stomach and along his left shoulder and up into his crushing chest, forcing him to fall limp onto the back of his seat.

'This is for Siân,' she said as he released an animalistic groan that reminded him of the sound

The Girls made while they were sucking in air, desperately trying to wrench off the torn clothing tied round their throats while he strangled them to death before burying them to avoid detection.

# PART THREE

# CARYS

*Brynmawr, Ebbw Vale, Wales, 2018*

I knew it was a bad idea the moment I stepped through the front door, but it was too late to turn back now. I could have but I disliked driving in the dark and the rain continued to slash against the single framed sash windows of the farmhouse. I was tired, and my muscles ached from padding through the gate in my hurry to reach the front door.

The place was eerie at night. I felt less alone knowing Gwenda was tucked up in bed just a quarter of a mile down the lane, but I also felt the ghosts of children nearby, and as I switched on the lights, they flickered into life just as the howling wind entered the chimney. It sounded like the cry of a baby.

No longer a warzone of publicity or the morbid destination for local dwellers to congregate, hoping to glimpse at The Murder House thinking they might capture the ghostly vision of one of The Girls, the desolate farm gave me chills.

Maybe it was a bad idea to tease the past into view by capturing glimpses of the history of the case, I thought, as I dumped my camera onto a stool and began to clear away folders of files littering the sofa. No, I wouldn't sit. Not yet. I had to keep busy or my thoughts would turn morose.

I made my way into the kitchen, stepping over discarded items from the boxes Lewis and I had packed but hadn't been able to take out to the bin.

Everything had been moved, the carpets stripped, and furniture piled up against the walls by CSI.

I should have booked myself into a B&B, but I didn't want to draw attention to myself again. I couldn't face reporters on my own. I reasoned that this time my purpose was to display to the world the lives shattered by crime. This was about the victims, not my father.

I slept fitfully on the sofa in the living room and awoke the following morning to a damp grey day. I'd received the phone call two days prior, assured DI Locke I could attend the unit, and instantly regretted it the moment I sat opposite her in the clinically clean, sparsely decorated room that reminded me of the one I dreamed about each night.

A body had been found beneath the concrete in Bill's basement. The one he used for dissecting the animals he would later stuff.

'Preliminary DNA analysis confirms that the bones discovered below the basement floor belong to Siân Kavanagh.'

The first thing that entered my head was, 'have you told Gwenda?'

'Officers visited her address earlier today to inform her.'

'I don't expect she took it well.'

DI Locke turned to DS Jones and asked him to leave. I sensed the moment the door closed behind him I was going to be interrogated, but the sensitive nature of the topic she wished to discuss made it clear to me they were stuck and were clutching for possible leads of inquiry to move their case along.

'How was your relationship with your father?'

'You mean did he sexually abuse me?'

'That's not what I was referring to, but as you've mentioned it, did he?'

I hadn't told DI Locke about the touching, the groping, the rapes. But I had given her a good enough reason to check Bill's basement. I hadn't told her that the visions and nightmares weren't about the basement inside my father's farmhouse at all, but were instead memories – real, not imagined – of Bill's lab where he sliced open and mounted birds of prey. Especially owls. The most haunting beady eyed creatures whose gaze followed me around the steel cold room. Where CSI found a hospital bed, a set of stirrups, and a four-piece leather strap set that looked like something from a US prison drama about incarcerated inmates awaiting the death penalty, but which came from the closure of a nearby asylum. He'd somehow nabbed an overhanging fluorescent lamp, pillows, sheets, a kidney jar, and various other frightening looking operating equipment.

Inside the property during their inspection, CSI had also discovered a medicine cabinet containing various pharmaceuticals, including ephedrine, a protected substance sometimes used by taxidermists to stiffen the floppy limbs of deceased animals before cutting them open to stuff with duck feathers, according to DI Locke.

Bill had been re-arrested at his address midway through the search. He was now being held in custody on remand after a psychological formulation proved him fit to await trial for the murders of Siân Kavanagh- whom detectives Locke and Jones suspected had been strangled with the T-shirt discovered wrapped around her neck during the excavation of the double concreted basement, and Bryn Howell. The syringe and a vial containing elements of the substance used to kill him discovered beneath his garden waste bin at the front of his house half a mile down the road from the farm, Gwenda's property stationed between them.

Gwenda had been questioned about the possibility that she'd supplied Bill with the drug and injecting equipment which had likely come from a hospital because the detectives had found no evidence to suggest Bill had purchased the controlled substance online via the Dark Net as they'd originally suspected. But she had conveniently struck a bad patch memory-wise and could not recall why she was seated in the interview room or remember who Bryn was.

She was dropped back home in an unmarked car where a social worker greeted her at the door, and surprisingly her memory returned intact for the full forty-five-minute consultation.

*Justice comes in many forms, Carys.*

DI Locke's voice cuts through my internal monologue. 'Carys? Your father, Bryn, did he-'

'You can't prove that's what happened to Seren unless you find her, which you haven't, have you?'

'Unfortunately, not.'

I'd read about fractured skulls indicating the impact of a fall or the victim being hit with a heavy object, symmetrical open cracks in bones around the torso provided evidence of stab wounds, bullet holes a shooting, and crushed larynx's proved strangulation. Cleverly constructed murder by poisoning an individual by injection it seemed wouldn't leave any evidence if all that was left was a skeleton. I expect DI Locke had no reason to argue that Bill Erwin had provided the fatal intoxicating jab to my father, but it seemed Gwenda had anticipated the possible discovery of Bryn's murder as a precaution to cover any potential link that might lead the police to her by continuing to display the symptoms of dementia that I now knew were fictitious.

The coroner was unlikely to gain permission to exhume my father's body so soon after his burial when the toxicology report conducted using the blood taken by his GP, also a trained phlebotomist, the morning he is said to have died was negative for all substances orally consumed, inhaled or otherwise, including it seemed his "medication."

Gwenda must have injected the ephedrine into his bloodstream hours after the GP had left. And by the time she had "found" him the drug had already been excreted from his system via the fluids that leaked from every orifice of his body.

That Gwenda had got away with murder didn't bother me as much as I presumed it would. Though I'd originally questioned her motive it seemed befitting, once I knew what my father had been capable of, that a sixty-three-year-old woman whose daughter had been raped by my father and murdered by his friend Bill, was the beneficiary of Bryn's estate.

If only she'd have inherited his land too. Considering I now had to go through the rigmarole of trying to find a buyer for it.

# GWENDA

*Brynmawr, Ebbw Vale, Wales, 2018*

She'd been using a fatal combination of beta-blockers and Metformin to poison him for some time, increasing the doses over the last few weeks and providing an intoxicating amount in the days since discovering Carys' diary but Bryn was stronger than he looked it appeared. Which was why she'd fixed him a deadly dose of ephedrine, ensuring he hadn't taken his "vitamins" for at least seven days before administering it.

It was far removed from the methodically thought-out revenge plan she'd had in mind, but those deep cutting words scored through her flesh, so she had to do something- now.

*Dear diary,*

*It happened again last night. The Shadow Man came to get me not long after I'd turned out the light. I know I wasn't asleep this time because I could feel his arms beneath me as he carried me down the steep stone steps into the lower part of the spaceship.*

*I don't know what was in the syringe, but it made me cold then numb. I was wide awake, but I couldn't move my arms or legs.*

*The strip-light flickered on and I squinted until my eyes adjusted to its piercing glare. The bulbs were large, round, and very bright.*

*I started to feel sick then.*

*The moment he raised my legs to snap the leather straps around my ankles my eyes felt heavy, and sleep came sudden and fast.*

*I woke up in bed this morning. The first thing I did was raise my arm to look at my wrist. But there were no marks there. Neither was there anything on my ankles.*

*I know it happened. It felt real. But how can I tell anyone if I have no proof?*

*Nobody believes a liar. And unfortunately, that's what everyone thinks I am. Bill made sure of that.*

*He was the one who spread the rumours about me*

*being a slag.*

*I know because that's what he called me once when I woke up on that bed in the room where the owl sat staring at me. He saw how frightened I was when I saw it, so he gave it to my father to watch over me while I slept. I tried getting rid of it, knocking it over, dragging it through the cornfield to get it clotted with mud so my mother would throw it out deeming it too dirty to salvage, but Bryn always brought it back, told me I was ungrateful. I haven't slept properly since. Because, like Bill said, it reminds me to stay quiet about the experiments.*

*He's fascinated with physiology, with death. In the owl's wide black eyes, I see Bill's. And when the moonlight catches it at the right angle, its flushed wings create long shadows on the walls of my bedroom, the feathers extend like arms reaching out to me, replicating a tall man.*

Gwenda felt sick at the knowledge that Bill had drugged Carys with her mother's medication to enable him to enact such disgusting things upon her flesh. But worse, she knew Bryn must have given his friends daughter the pills from Rhiannon's stash which meant they must have been working together.

Bryn and Bill were co-offenders. Carys was their victim. But what if she wasn't the only one?

# CARYS

*Brynmawr, Ebbw Vale, Wales, 2018*

After heaving boxes from the house and carrying rubbish bags back and forth across the path, dumping them alongside the space where the second skip had been delivered, I sat down to admire my work. I'd cleaned away the grime and grease from the kitchen, wiped down the mouldy windows, swept the floor, vacuumed the carpets, scrubbed the bathroom, and mopped the linoleum.

Lewis' car crawled down the narrow gritty path and stopped just short of the gate. He didn't want to see the house. Had made that very clear. After I'd sat down and read my diary from first to last page before handing it over to DI Locke, I'd called him in tears, breaking down into sobs the moment he answered my call.

'Carys, what the hell is going on?'

I hadn't prepared to tell him over the phone, but the distance it gave us allowed me to offload my hideous childhood experiences to Lewis without having to visually witness his reaction. It was difficult, but it would have been far harder had I seen his facial expressions and not only heard the pain in his voice over the images of my abuse he imagined as I recounted those lost years, the breakthrough that Bill's arrest had given me, the memories I had recovered since daring myself to read the diary that contained everything I'd been denying for years.

He listened, acknowledged, then said, 'I'm coming to get you.'

'No, there's something I must do first.'

'Carys?' I could hear the desperation in his voice.

'The funeral. I'm going.'

'Siân's?'

'Yes. I know I don't owe her anything, but Gwenda doesn't have anyone.'

'I understand,' he said curtly. He didn't but at least he was trying. 'When is it?'

'Friday.'

We spoke every night all week, sometimes past

midnight, for hours. Sharing our hopes, our fears, and swapping stories of our childhood that enabled me to fit the good amongst the bad to create a somewhat unreliable but more coherent narrative than perhaps I would have been able to develop had I not received that phone call from Gwenda eight months before, informing me of my father's death.

I'd stood that afternoon with the late summer sun on my back, my skin glowing from the trips across the garden with piles of unwanted items that thankfully contained none of my own memories. Watching the things that only mattered to my parents crash into the skip, clanging against the metal, and disappear amongst the piles of clutter. It was therapeutic.

Lewis walked toward me, arms outstretched, drawing them back, unsure for a moment if I felt comfortable enough to allow him to pull me close, to hold me. I pressed my body against his and breathed in his familiar cologne. Felt our hearts beating out of sync against one another's chests. Felt the stab of pain in my spine as I released him. My body slowly becoming whole, my feelings returning.

It would take time the psychotherapist said. The one I'd spoken to, having been given the number for her after accepting the PWP's referral. I was planning on starting the next chapter of my life the following Tuesday at 1:00pm, in the same backstreet room of the Clifton clinic we'd meet in after lunch every week until I didn't need counselling anymore. I was apprehensive, but I knew the timing was right. If I didn't go through with it now, I might never have the optimism or internal strength to begin my healing journey at all.

Siân's funeral was held in a quaint cemetery several miles outside of Abergavenny, paid for using some of the inheritance Gwenda had received from my father's solicitor.

The sky was gloomy, gulls fluttered in droves across the skyline, heading for the sea. The minister's words floated through my ears, the melodic hymns distracting me from the sad truth that we were alone in the chapel, except for DI Locke and DS Jones, who'd attended, I felt, out of a sense of duty, to lay the case to rest. But also, because I think out of respect, feeling compassion for The Girl's whose lives had been cut short by the actions of two awful excuses for the term "men."

Leaving the chapel, arm linked through Gwenda's,

a symbol of solidarity, of friendship, and reassurance that I would remain silent, this time by choice, over her version of "divine intervention" by assisting my father into deaths waiting arms, I caught sight of a familiar face between the trees.

I lay a hand on Gwenda's arm and told her I was going to use the toilet. I turned toward the chapel, leaving her talking to the detectives. I headed for the treeline and walked round the path toward the headstone, but the ground was empty.

It couldn't be her. Seren was dead. Had never made it to adulthood. But the vision of the woman I was positive I'd seen was an adult version of the girl I'd witnessed climbing into my father's light blue car all those years ago.

The boys were out when we arrived back in Bristol.

Lewis brought my backpack from the boot of the car, carrying it over one shoulder. The base of the landline flickered red alerting me to a voicemail. I pressed the button and listened to the estate agent who informed me he was going to use the set of keys I'd had cut and delivered to him the previous day to enter the farm and take photos, hoping to list the house on their website the following morning. I called back to confirm that it was okay and entered the kitchen to pour myself a cup of coffee. Sinking down onto the sofa in the living room ten minutes later to drink it.

'The house is going to be put on the market tomorrow.'

'I heard,' he said. 'It's good,' said Lewis.

'Yes, it is.' I took a swig of my coffee and swallowed.

'You're okay with it?'

'Relieved would be a better word.' I smiled.

Lewis sat beside me, draped an arm over my shoulder, fumbling with the remote in one hand, and switched on the television.

'. . . the tragic murders of Amelia Holbrooke, Ella James, and her infant daughter. A witness by the name of Catherine Appleby has come forward to say that Bryn Howell attempted to drag her into his car, sometime in 1992. She believes she was extremely lucky not to have been abducted. Detective Inspector Locke stated that had she been, Catherine may not be alive today. Police suspect Mr Howell was also responsible for the disappearance of Seren Lloyd, whose body was not found on the property and is yet to be located. Bryn Howell's close friend, Bill Erwin's, trial begins in September. Despite evidence proving him responsible for the abduction and murder of Siân Kavanagh, whose remains were discovered below the re-concreted basement of his home, Mr Erwin has pleaded not guilty . . .'

Lewis looked at me and reached out to hold my hand. I squeezed his back.

I didn't want to put myself through the tough criminal court system, so I refrained from pressing charges against Bill for the abuse I suffered at his hands. But my statement would be used as a character profile during the trial, proving Bill's motive was sexual, despite Siân's remains being too damaged and decayed to provide definitive proof of his motivation to kill her.

Should Bill be found guilty by the jury, forensics proved he'd murdered my father by injecting him with ephedrine using the syringe discovered beneath his waste bin though they hadn't yet been able to prove from where he purchased the drug, because of course *he* didn't. It was likely he'd be sentenced for at least one of his crimes. His defence barrister had a fight on her hands either way.

DI Locke and DS Jones were attending court and had told me, although I was not technically considered a victim in the eyes of the law, that as a witness they would keep me updated on the day's activities.

I could have attended Cardiff Crown Court, but I'd decided not to sit up in the public gallery and listen to Bill recount lie after lie. My counsellor suggested on the phone that it might provide me with some element of closure, but, like I said to DI Locke, I only wanted to hear the words: 'he's been sentenced to x amount of years in prison.'

I expected Bill to play on his age-related symptoms and the judge to consider the time he had left on earth before deciding on his fate, but I was positive he'd be sentenced to at least a few years in prison. Bill deserved to know how it felt to have your freedom snatched from you. With the time to reflect on his actions I hoped he'd learn to accept that what he'd done was wrong, maybe even regret his behaviour.

The sky had cleared above the Victorian houses on the opposite side of the road. I watched a butterfly circle the window several times before fluttering toward the honeysuckle and setting up camp there. I released my grip on Lewis' hand, took the remote control from his other, switched off the television, and turned his face to mine. He leant in close and kissed me tenderly.

I had no more revelations to disclose to my husband.

After DI Locke told me she needed Iefan's consent to pass on details of his biology from the mouth swab the doctor had taken from him at the CID unit during the initial stages of the investigation, I stole his razor along with Lewis' toothbrush and paid a private company to test the DNA from some of his facial hair. Iefan's was a 99.99% positive match to his father, Lewis.

To say that I was stunned would be a huge understatement, but I supposed in hindsight the heavy blood loss I'd experienced during those first few weeks of my first trimester must have been a miscarriage. Continuing to have unprotected sex with Lewis had resulted in the pregnancy of our eldest son when I'd thought I was still pregnant with my father's child. I could only guess his low birth weight and the midwife's exclamation that he was 'four weeks premature' was after all, correct. He must have inherited more of my paternal bloodline than Rhys, which was why I had wrongly assumed Iefan was biologically Bryn's.

I love my boys both the same, but I must admit the news brought some peace of mind I didn't know until I'd discovered it, was missing.

'I suppose we'd better get started on packing up and repainting this place,' said Lewis, eyes roaming the living room of our home. 'Now that the farm is up for sale there's nothing preventing us from looking at houses. We should get close to the asking price for this, which means we'll be mortgage-free.'

I nodded and leant my head to rest on his shoulder. Nothing was going to stop me from doing anything now I had the chance to move on.

*Nothing except yourself,* said my conscience.

*I'm working on it.*

I didn't care where we lived so long as it was nowhere near Brynmawr. I could set up a studio anywhere, though I doubted I'd be able to find an assistant as loyal as Sharon.

I'd already stored away the photographs I'd taken from our visit together to Ebbw Vale. The only project

I had ongoing, was me. It would take time and work and was an assignment far more challenging than any I'd previously undertaken, but I knew I had the emotional strength because with Lewis and the boys by my side, I felt as though I could achieve anything.

# SEREN

*Brynmawr, Ebbw Vale, Wales, 2018*

Seren had followed the investigation from her Manchester studio flat in the centre of the city. A glacial monstrosity overlooking a noughties-built housing estate with a view of both the skyline and the surrounding playing field below which belonged to the local secondary school. She'd viewed the pictures of the farm online. Had called the estate agents as soon as she recognised the "vintage spacious farm" advertised to include four acres of land and two outbuildings: a stable and a barn.

The place had been left to ruin. The owners (Bryn Howell and his wife Rhiannon) hadn't bothered to re-supply the land the police had guarded while it was being dug up. Mounds of earth was still visible in one of the photographs. But she didn't care. It wasn't the land she wanted. It was the house.

She'd made an offer for the full asking price and within an hour she received a phone call to say that the vendor had accepted. With no mortgage required the sale would take approximately three months. But because the titleholder was deceased, and the probate file had already gone through months before, a quick sale was possible. With some back and forth between solicitors she'd become the legal homeowner of Ty Mynydd (mountain house) – she presumed was named due to the distant view of sugar-loaf mountain – on Llangynidr Road in Brynmawr, eight weeks later.

Despite using a pseudonym and requesting her bid remain anonymous – her National Insurance number non-existent and owning no official ID of her own – she knew the moment she received the deeds the police would come knocking. Although the house had been purchased using the money in Anne-Marie's bank account the land documents were registered to her as Seren Lloyd. She used her recently obtained driving licence, approved with her student card and her solicitors signature on the back of her passport sized photo, so it was only a matter of days before that occurred.

She hit the road the second she'd signed the contract and belted it down the M6 motorway, passing through Birmingham, Gloucester, and hitting the A4042 to Ebbw Vale in three and a half hours. The place she hadn't seen in twenty-four years. To collect the keys from the estate agent who waited in the lane for her as instructed.

She parked the white Ford Transit directly in front of the bins, far enough away from the house that when the flames reached out, they wouldn't lick it and set it alight.

She took the keys from the agents outstretched hand, thanked him, and waited for him to return to his car and drive away before she opened the boot and carried two petrol cannisters filled to the brim up to the front door, leaving them on the porch step while she went inside.

She took a quick glance right into the living room and down the hall to where the kitchen was situated before stopping in front of the door that led to the basement where Bryn had told her she could sit inside to eat sweets the day he'd taken her.

She turned the key and flicked on the light.

Trudging down the steps, she felt the brush of a spider's leg that hung from a web fall across her arm. She brushed it aside. Nothing scared her anymore. Years of therapy, learning to trust others, and to love herself again had taught her that fear is a reaction to anger. When she began to release the hurt that she felt over her abduction, the sexual assault, and the beating she endured before Bryn had strangled her and left her for dead, she relinquished her need to defend herself against things, including spiders. Her fear of the dark, of enclosed spaces, of men, and her phobia of insects, having woken up on the ground with bugs crawling all over her, face swollen, naked accept for her vest and knickers, dress gone, bruises around her throat from where Bryn's hands had been before he'd disappeared, opening her eyes to see him through the trees returning with a spade intending to bury her, had all become a distant memory. One she often relived at night. Over the years she'd learned to deal with it, accept it as a part of her past, while continuing to live each day that came, one at a time, like her therapist had taught her.

She allowed the memory of her escape to play. Pushing it away only made it strong enough to overpower her, and she'd vowed never to let that happen again as she took a quick glance down to her scarred wrists.

*

Her eyes flickered open. She felt ants in her frilly white socks. A ladybird tickled her hand. She dragged herself upright, head spinning, throat sore, mouth crusted with blood.

She'd somehow stood on trembling legs, forced herself onward. Kept her heartrate even by willing herself to keep moving.

*Don't stop, Seren*, said the small voice within her, pushing her forth. *He'll be back in a minute to bury you.*

She strode forward, quickened her pace, until the trees became one long blur of green. She ran through the undergrowth, calves burning as her muscles stretched. She picked up speed as the earth flattened out, and by the time she'd made it onto the bypass, flagging down a speeding vehicle she didn't recognise, she felt, for the first time in days, in control of her body, her future.

She couldn't go back home. Didn't want to worry her parents. Didn't want to endure medical examinations in a hospital bed. Didn't want to sit in a small room while being questioned by the police about what Bryn had done to her, where he'd touched her.

She felt sick, her chest burned, but she kept going, following the A-road onto the dual carriageway until she could walk no more. She raised her hand in mid-air as she fell to the ground, slumped onto her side, exhausted. The camper pulled over onto the hard shoulder. A kind faced woman leapt from the vehicle and bolted toward her. 'Get help!' she shrieked to someone over her shoulder.

She shook her head, began to cry.

The woman carried Seren with the help of her boyfriend into the back of the camper van. It was bigger inside than how it looked on the outside. A complete home on wheels, thought Seren, drifting in and out of wakefulness.

'I'm Anne-Maire,' said the woman once they were seated inside the van. Pointing to the man she added, 'this is Matthew.' She paused, waiting for Seren to name herself, to explain why she'd been running along the verge of the dual carriageway wearing only underwear and covered in mud and bruises with a cut lip. It came out thick and fast. 'Sienna,' she said, jaw aching from the effort of speech. 'I was kidnapped.'

Anne-Marie's eyes widened. 'Oh, my god. Who by? What did they do to you? Oh, my poor love. Matthew, we've got to do something. Call the police. An ambulance. Drive her to the hospital . . .'

Seren began to wail then, 'no, no, no. Please. I can't. They'll send me back.'

'Won't your parents be looking for you?' said Anne-Marie.

'You don't understand, I can't go back. Ever. I won't. I'll run away-'

Seren had given Anne-Marie a false name to temporarily throw her off the very public scent of who she really was. Had unknowingly suggested it was her parents she was afraid of.

Matthew shushed her. 'She's traumatised. Why don't we drive her back to ours? We can sort all this out later. Get her something to eat and drink. She looks tired.'

Anne-Marie nodded, gripped Seren's hand tight.

364

'You'll be okay, girl. We'll take care of you.'

But that day became night. Then another. And another. Seren learned that Anne-Marie and Matthew were desperate for a child of their own, hadn't been able to make one themselves. They fed and clothed her. Bought her books to read. Agreed it was probably for the best she wasn't being schooled. Nodded when she said she'd had enough of being told what to do. They soothed her when she woke up screaming in the night, the terror of her abduction replaying itself in her sleep. They travelled the country, rarely involved themselves in politics and didn't own a television. It wasn't difficult for them to keep her away from the media. They weren't the sort of people to draw attention to themselves.

Matthew worked in the army. He was away a lot. Leaving Seren and Anne-Marie to form a bond she didn't feel she had with her workaholic, hair obsessed mother or her lying cheating father. She missed them sometimes, but not having to witness her parents worry and sadness made it easier to pretend that one day, when she was older, she could return home. That they'd frozen in time, that her friends wouldn't have grown up, got married or had kids of their own by the time she'd gained the courage to face them again.

When Matthew lost both the lower ends of his legs in Afghanistan and was given early retirement on health grounds, Anne-Marie applied to the council for them to be rehoused somewhere suitable for a wheelchair bound man of forty-four. They were offered a one-bedroom terrace in Liverpool.

By then Seren was old enough to work. She'd used the name Sienna for years, but when Anne-Marie offered to allow her the use of their surname she was able to apply to college to save up for a place of her own to rent so she wouldn't have to sleep on the sofa in the living room slash dining room of their small abode, because of course they couldn't put her name on the tenancy because no one in a position of authority was supposed to know they had a daughter.

Seren studied for a BTEC in childcare. Went on to train in child psychology at The University of Liverpool. Secured a job for the Child and Adolescent Mental Health Service in Manchester. Bought the studio flat with the wages she'd saved plus some money from Matthew's army retirement fund, as he was also entitled to disability benefits. And for the past two years she'd been supporting children and young people with autism.

She wanted to help those in greater need than she might once have required had she not flagged that camper van down and made the brave decision to trust another human being after the horrors she'd endured in Bryn Howell's basement for those three awful days of her life. Her childhood innocence lost in just seventy-two hours.

*

She glanced round the basement, remembering the awful things she'd experienced in there. When she was ready, she retreated upstairs, slammed shut the door, locked it, and turned toward the entrance where she thought she caught sight of a fleeing shadow.

Must be the clouds overhead shadowing the ground she told herself, collecting the first petrol cannister from the floor, turning the lid and letting it drop to the carpet. She poured the petrol over the floor, enjoyed the sloshing sound it made. She splashed it over the kitchen units, over the carpet in the living room, then up the stairs. There wasn't much need to cover the first floor because gravity would drag the fire up the staircase via the wooden bannister, through the ceiling via the polystyrene tiles, and up into the cavity walls. But she opened a few windows in the bedrooms to allow the oxygen to ventilate throughout the house to assist the flames anyway.

She prised off the lid of the second petrol cannister and held it away from her as she lit a piece of discarded paper she found on the lawn. She walked slowly backwards until she was stood on the concrete step at the front of the house. Once the flame had sufficiently begun to burn the paper black and blue, she dropped it onto the mat in the porch and stood aside while she drew her arm back and swung the cannister into the house.

Some of the fuel would seep out onto the carpet, but the rest would cause the unsealed container to draw in enough air to blow. And when it did, she expected the windows to shatter so she ran from the building, across the soft green grass, and down to where her van was parked, watching the six-inch flames follow one another like a giant snake. Down the hallway, splitting in two mid-way along the floor and trailing into the kitchen and living room. Up the kitchen units, the staircase.

The plastic petrol cannister on the floor several feet down the hall was already melting around the edges when she escaped to her vehicle.

She heard a supersonic *boom*. The building lit up orange and red and black.

She felt a hand on her shoulder and flinched, ducking at the same time as she heard the distinctive sound of glass smashing. She turned away from the crackling, spitting flames to meet the eyes of Gwenda Kavanagh. Siân's mother. The woman whose face was plastered across newspapers countrywide.

A moment of recognition danced across her eyes before they beamed, and she smiled.

She felt Gwenda's hand clench tighter around her bony flesh and together they watched the farmhouse burn until the flames died, leaving just plumes of chugging black smoke to fill the sky.

They remained standing there in silence for a while until Gwenda said, 'are you okay?'

'Yes,' she said. 'I am now.'

'Tell me you didn't spend two hundred and eighty thousand pounds on a house just so you could burn it to the ground?'

'Okay, I won't.'

Gwenda smiled. Seren laughed and squeezed the woman's hand tighter. Tears of relief sliding down her cheeks.

# AUTHOR'S NOTE

In August 2017 The Children's Charity published their findings from a year-long report detailing the reasons given by young people reported missing from care in their Return Home Debriefs with officers, when found. Out of the estimated 100,000 children who go missing every year, 4,500 from Wales, approximately 3,750 of them return. Some have run away due to the strain of living with the after-effects of growing up in an abusive or neglectful household. However, most are preyed upon by adults and sexually exploited long before they leave home or disappear. Unfortunately, we may never know the motives for the proportion of children who do not return.

Although The Knowledge GAP report conducted by the charity which included professionals from the police and social services focussed non-exclusively on children and young people in care, I was shocked to discover these figures. And this lesser known information got me thinking about what it might have been like for the families of those left behind.

Researching false memory as part of my university studies for a psychology degree I came across the fascinating yet little known phenomenon of False Abduction Syndrome, or FAS. Manifesting itself with symptoms such as: déjà vu, sleep paralysis, insomnia, lucid dreams, childhood amnesia, and misremembered facts, the disorder can become, in its extreme form, a life-limiting psychological condition. Evidence suggests it often exhibits itself in sufferers who re-experience a traumatic event such as repeated sexual abuse leading to symptoms of complex trauma.

The idea for this novel as most of my crime fiction is borne stemmed from the literature I discovered when entering forensic psychology training. Reading case vignettes from individuals who claim to have been abducted by aliens and absorbing the vast quantity of teaching materials on abnormal and parapsychology.

Psychologists are still trying to understand how false memories work, but false abduction has gained considerable attention in recent years due to the recently acquired knowledge gained from the testimonies of individuals who have experienced both childhood sexual abuse and state their nightly visitations from extra-terrestrials are in fact their abusers in disguise through narrative self-analysis.

Our memories of traumatic episodes are often vague because during the event the brain subconsciously processes events we experience while attempting to consciously attend to the threat to our self that we perceive. What this means is that when activated during a stressful situation, the threat of sexual violence for instance, the parts of our brain which urge us to fight, flee from, or freeze against our opponent to preserve our lives overrides the environmental material we process.

This act of denial is an unconscious (automatic) process we have little control over. In its extreme sufferers can exhibit symptoms of dissociation. However, what this means is that when confronted with triggering material (the sight, sound, smell, taste, or touch of something that our subconscious associates with the trauma) sensory overload can occur, forcing our conscious mind to react. This is where memories come in the form of flashbacks or nightmares.

Weeks, months, or even years later, to help us cope

with the trauma our brains may allow us to remember small snippets of information we were not aware we subconsciously processed during the traumatic event. When sensory knowledge (sight, sound, smell, taste, touch) is too difficult to contend with our brains remap themselves, a bit like a car's Engine Control Unit, by re-evaluating and re-assigning the traumatic material.

I was interested to know how the progression of FAS as a psychological disorder would manifest itself if the individual sufferer had discovered her father might have been a serial killer, triggering her own memories of child sexual abuse.

How does it feel to acknowledge you were the victim of something so horrific by a family member? How does mental ill health affect close relationships? How do heinous crimes such as the rape-murder of children affect the families left behind?

Although the theme of incest is rather dark, I have tried my utmost to write about it with authenticity and with admiration and respect for those who have sadly been betrayed by the people who are supposed to protect them from such atrocities.

While attempting to cover the subject as

emotionally realistically as possible I have also tried not to include any gratuitous violence.

I am a pedant when it comes to procedural timelines, and I always try to ensure that while the novel is compelling to read, the plot remains factual. The DNA analysis of human bones can be completed within days, but when resources are scarce may take a couple of weeks to officially report. Forensic anthropologists can determine the sex, race, height, age, and weight of human remains, but without the help of odontologists (employed to determine the identification of an individual by their teeth), or pathologists (to determine the cause of death), clothing fibres discovered at the secondary scene cannot be used by forensic scientists to glean intelligence which is used to estimate the place of death, also known as the primary crime scene. Because of this, I had to choose a burial site close to the perpetrators place of residence (in this instance on his own land) so that rather than fall fowl of providing lengthy descriptions of police procedure I could focus on the characters and their motives to steer the story forward. I hope you can forgive me this small act of poetic licence.

If you would like to read more information about the themes in this title, please see:

https://www.childrenssociety.org.uk/news-and-blogs/our-blog/wales-missing-children

https://www.childrenssociety.org.uk/what-we-do/resources-and-publications/the-knowledge-gap-safeguarding-missing-children-in-wales

https://www.walesonline.co.uk/news/wales-news/shocking-figures-show-hundreds-wales-13369630

https://www.psychologytoday.com/gb/articles/200303/alien-abductions-the-real-deal

https://thepsychologist.bps.org.uk/volume-19/edition-6/recovered-and-false-memories

# ACKNOWLEDGEMENTS

I'd like to say a huge thank you, firstly, to my long-suffering husband Michael, whose encouragement and advice are unconditional.

A special mention must go to the men and women who work for or with the United Kingdom Police Service, putting their lives on the line each day to protect the public in their fight against crime.

I received invaluable advice from several professionals whose areas of expertise included: forensic anthropology, pathology, forensic science, and odontology to ensure the procedural aspects of this title were written as realistically as possible. I would not have been able to do this without the selfless detectives working for Blaenau Gwent Police. Although Detective Inspector Locke and her colleague Detective Sergeant Jones are fictitious character's I hope I have given the real Murder Investigation Teams working for BGP justice.

For the support they offer hybrid author's like myself, I must thank the entire blogging community who review and promote our titles. I am extremely grateful. I couldn't do it without you. I would especially like to thank my publicist, Caroline Vincent.

I must thank my early readers for their objective honest literary criticism which continues to inspire my writing. Particularly my champion: Kerry Watts, Billy McLaughlin, and Amanda Oughton.

And, lastly, I offer a huge thank you to my readers all over the world who have purchased my titles and for believing in me. Reviews are important to us, it helps other readers to find our work, so please share your thoughts, and recommend this title to a friend.

Please help other readers to find my work by leaving a review on Amazon.co.uk/Amazon.com and Goodreads.

https://www.amazon.co.uk/Louise-Mullins/e/B00J0LYBKU

https://www.amazon.com/Louise-Mullins/e/B00J0LYBKU

https://www.goodreads.com/author/show/7484872.Louise_Mullins

Purchase Kindle and paperback copies of all my titles here:

https://www.louisemullinsauthor.com/

Be the first to hear about new releases by 'liking' my Facebook author page:

https://www.facebook.com/LouiseMullinsAuthor/

where you can sign up to review titles before they are published and enter competitions to win signed copies of my books.

You can also follow me on Twitter where I regularly post book reviews:

https://twitter.com/MullinsAuthor

Printed in Great Britain
by Amazon

47541885R00220